WESTERN LITERATURE SERIES

BREATHE SOMETHING *nice*

STORIES BY

Emily Hammond

UNIVERSITY OF NEVADA PRESS

RENO / LAS VEGAS

WESTERN LITERATURE SERIES

University of Nevada Press, Reno, Nevada 89557 USA
Copyright © 1997 by Emily Hammond
All rights reserved
Manufactured in the United States of America
Book design by Carrie Nelson House
Library of Congress Cataloging-in-Publication Data
Hammond, Emily.
Breathe something nice : stories / Emily Hammond.
p. cm. — (Western literature series)
ISBN 0-87417-293-4 (pbk: alk. paper)
I. Title. II. Series.
PS3558.A44892B74 1997   96-47665
813'.54-dc21 CIP

01   00   99   98   97   5   4   3   2

FOR MY HUSBAND,
STEVEN

CONTENTS

ACKNOWLEDGMENTS

The author acknowledges the original publishers of these stories: "Breathe Something Nice" in *American Fiction*; "The Grand Tour" in *Puerto Del Sol*; "My Marilyn" in *Fiction*; "Polaroid" in *Crazyhorse*; "Swift and Maine" in *Nimrod*; "Why Would a Man" in *Prism International* (also anthologized in *Henfield Prize Stories*); and "Wicked" in *New England Review*.

Grateful acknowledgment is made to the Henfield Foundation and the Colorado Council on the Arts. Special thanks also to Robert Boswell, Antonya Nelson, Jonathan Penner, C. E. Poverman, and Steven Schwartz.

SWIFT AND MAINE

Swift and Maine, Swift and Maine. As a child I pulled the covers over my head and said that to myself while falling asleep, the names of the babysitters my brothers and I liked the best. Eudora Swift and Mamie Maine. But we called them Swift and Maine. That's what they called each other.

Swift and Maine — it sounded like a railroad, like a train traveling fast across a snowbound prairie. I was sure they came from someplace exotic, New England or Canada. No, my father said last night; we had a long talk about Swift and Maine. No, they came from Arizona or Utah, someplace like that.

Our parents went out a lot when we were children, dinner parties and cocktail parties, tailgate parties, skeet shooting, duck hunting. And so it would be Swift and Maine for a night, a weekend, a week sometimes, Swift and Maine with their little bitty hands and big stomachs, plump thighs tucked into woolen dresses.

They sewed, they knitted. We should've been bored but we were in love. Swift was losing her teeth and smiled daintily to conceal it; Maine was losing her hair and would bend over to show us her emerging pink scalp. Swift and Maine taught us how to bake and cook, the mysteries of the kitchen, pies and buns and tiny chickens called game hens.

"Now, they could cook," my father said last night. "Remember their chili and cornbread?"

He's divorced now and so am I, though much more recently. That's why I'm staying here, till I get back on my feet. Three days ago I showed up unexpectedly and my father took me in, put me up in the spare room where he stores old newspapers. I asked him last night if he thought Swift and Maine were ever married.

"Not that I know of," he said. "They were together, as long as we knew them they were always together. They knew each other as girls, they said. Grew up in the same town and left together for California. They shared rooms, that's how they put it. Shared rooms."

■ Our parents divorced years ago. My brothers and I stayed with our father, while our mother went off to live in Tunisia with her new husband, a wealthy importer-exporter; we're still not quite sure what he does. I asked my father once why they divorced, a question that made him laugh. "Your mother," he said, "was a clotheshorse."

He never remarried. Once we grew up, he moved into this place, a thirties-style townhouse with banana trees growing all around. Inside there's a lot of mahogany paneling and a dumbwaiter and a buzzer under the dining room table for the maid. There is no maid, but my father pretends. Gerta, he calls her. "Gerta!" he says while opening a can of soup. "Some luncheon, please, Gerta!"

My father, when I was a child, seemed always to be parading around the house in costume: jodhpurs, or a duck-hunting jacket, or a tuxedo. Now he wears flannel shirts and spends all day in the leather recliner he calls the humpback whale. He reads newspapers from small towns, places he's never been. He's delighted by local elections, the squabbling of city councils and school boards, the personalities. There's Assistant

Mayor Birdy Finer in Cut Bank, Montana, for instance, or Bobby Murphy of Winnesset, Massachusetts, of Winnesset *Weekly* fame, who wants to start a museum to honor the town's first and only industry — chair legs.

"Swift and Maine liked a good laugh," my father said last night. "Remember the goat?"

The goat! Swift and Maine brought my father a goat for his birthday, as a joke; they borrowed it from a friend of theirs. As my father stood with his hands over his eyes, they led the goat from their car, a big red ribbon around its neck, and personally laid the animal in my father's arms. It nibbled at his tie. The goat ate all the flowers in our yard that afternoon while my brothers and I danced after it, feeding it more flowers. My father laughed, Swift and Maine laughed, and I knew they were family. Their pictures were in our scrapbooks. They came to the hospital the day I was born. They took turns holding me.

I'm here at my father's because I don't know what I'm doing. He fixed up the spare room for me: a nightstand and a single bed with a pillow like hardtack.

"Don't you have any other pillows?" I asked him.

"No," he said.

On the floor by my bed is a box of childhood things he thought I might like to see — dolls from different countries in their native dress, and a stuffed cow with a pink udder. By the box is my suitcase, half unpacked. I was putting clothes away last night when it occurred to me I was *putting them away.* As if I'm staying here forever. The thought comforted but shocked me, and I stopped unpacking.

"A daddy's girl," I said to my father last night. "Is that what you want, an old maid? Kick me out, don't let me stay here. Kick me out."

"Go," he said. "Or stay. But only as long as you want to, not any longer."

He got up and weaved out of the room. We'd been drinking shots of whiskey. That's when it started, the talk about Swift and Maine.

"Remember Swift and Maine?" I hollered after him.

He came back into the room. "That's funny," he said and poured us both another shot. "I was just going to ask you the same thing."

■ We stayed up till dawn talking about Swift and Maine. That was last night. Tonight I'm on the phone with my ex-husband. "What do you remember most?" I say.

"Your talking and laughing in your sleep. One night you sat up in bed yelling 'tax credits, tax credits!'"

I remember nights when I woke up unable to breathe. I thought there was someone walking around the room, touching things on my bureau, a man or a woman, I couldn't tell which.

"Frank," I say. After all these years I still can't get over his name, so stolid, so silly. Frankly Frank. "I'll call you next week, okay?"

"Dana, you've got to stop calling."

"Five years, Frank. *Five years.*" I hang up and look around me at this room, the phone room. An entire small room devoted to the making of phone calls. A cane chair, a desk built into the wall, an old black telephone with a withered cord.

For five years Frank and I were close friends, tentative lovers. Lovers, yes, but similar to a child bride and a child groom left alone together on the wedding night — a shyness that, with us, never went away. Doomed to go on together as pleasant traveling companions, yet unable to go anywhere but the known corners of our house.

"It's nice you and Frank are so agreeable and cooperative," my lawyer said once. "But why? It's not natural."

"What's natural?" I said. "We were kind to each other. We didn't fight."

The separation was my idea. Only I couldn't bring myself to move out of the house, so I moved into another room. "Like roommates," Frank said, and our eyes met. I moved out within the week.

"It's more natural," my lawyer said last week, "to go at each other's throats." Then he asked me out.

He took me to a French restaurant and, later, kissed me at my door. I kissed him back and dug my nails into his suede jacket. It felt good, like biting down on leather to ease the pain.

"What are you doing?" he said.

I looked at my hand. "I don't know. Goodnight," I said. "Call me."

The next day I threw everything into a suitcase and came to my father's, where I hid under a quilt and thought about Frank and dreamed of petting zoos and children's TV shows staged by nice men in suspenders and baggy pants with funny caps on their heads.

That was three days ago. I'm still under the quilt, only now I'm hiding in the phone room, hungover and thinking about last night, how I raved on and on about Swift and Maine like a lunatic. "It was just after Christmas, remember Dad? You said, 'Let's drop in on Swift and Maine.' I was a senior in high school, I hadn't seen them in years. So we brought them fruitcake and shortbread; you remembered they were crazy about shortbread. Swift answered the door and said 'Oh my' and called back to Maine, and we all hugged and kissed. Swift had this perfect smile, like a toothpaste commercial. False teeth. And Maine must've gone bald because she was wearing a wig, remember? We sat on the couch and had tea and that's when I saw it, the walker. You couldn't miss it. It was right out in the middle of the room like a piece of furniture. They asked all the usual questions, how was school and did I have a beau, and had I decided on a college yet. How were the boys. You said they weren't boys but as tall as basketball players and traveling through Africa at the moment. All I could do was stare at the walker. Why the walker? I kept secretly glancing at their legs. They looked all right to me. Maybe it wasn't the idea of the walker so much — after all, they were old — but the fact nobody mentioned it. But it was right there, like somebody sitting with us. I could've reached out and touched it. I sat there with this nervous frozen look on my face; I couldn't follow the conversation. I kept seeing the walker and thinking about Maine not having any hair, and her wig. Was it the good kind or one of those stretchy things they advertise in the TV guide, like a bathing cap with hair on it? And Swift's teeth. Her gums. Were they smooth like a baby's? Did she have any teeth left at all, maybe just one? How did she put them in, the teeth? I've never known that. How do they make them stay put? Glue? They must use glue —"

"Get to the point," my father said.

So I broke down and cried about Frank until the sun came up, while my father rubbed my shoulders and handed me Kleenex. Finally, around seven, I went to bed. On the way to my room I passed the hallway mirror, an unmerciful sun shining on it. I looked like a wreck, but smart somehow, my eyes swollen and liquid and my hair slicked back, like a muskrat or a mongoose or some other low-to-the-ground, sharp, knowing animal.

■ I'm dragging the quilt behind me like an old friend, down the hallway and into the den where my father is reading. I glance at his paper, the Lodi *Sentinel*. "Any good news?"

"In Lodi," he says, "the citizens are restless. Some people want to close down the zoo till improvements are made. But the city won't give the zoo any more money; they want to up the sales tax instead. There's this guy quoted. 'The animals aren't happy,' he says. 'They're in cages. They need more space.' 'They're animals,' somebody else says. 'Born in captivity. They don't know anything else and taxpayers aren't going to stand for it. The zoo is not a priority.'"

I pull up a footstool, a horrid little footstool that makes me think I'm in a Dickens novel. "Where did you get this thing?" I say.

"Your mother. One of those things she didn't want."

My mother once told me, during one of her infrequent visits, that my father had made passes at all her friends. I was fourteen. I confronted my father. "Why the hell not?" he said. "Your mother was too busy trying on shoes." But he laughed as he said it, and I was never quite sure if he meant it or not.

"Dad?"

"Yes, Dana." From behind the newspaper.

"Don't you get lonely?"

"I'm too old," he says.

"You are not." No answer. "Swift and Maine," I say. "Do you think they were lovers?"

"Maybe. Maybe not. I don't know. Didn't we already talk about this?"

"Last night, yes." I like to think of them in bed together, biting each other at the nape of the neck, doing somersaults in their Swift and Maine way.

Still, I'm sad. Sad but warm. Like the day of my wedding and the day of my divorce, the sweetness and sorrow of people moving on. Once, when our parents were away, Swift and Maine and my brothers and I baked cookies. Not just any cookies, but the kind you put through this contraption that Swift and Maine had brought along, a cookie press. You'd stuff the dough into the chute, and crank: out would come a rectangular cookie with ridges on its back, which you sprinkled with sugar. I ate lots of dough and too many cookies, and later that night woke up sick. My skin was clammy, my throat so full I couldn't cry out. I got up and wandered around the house, traveling through dark rooms to the one light, the kitchen, where Swift and Maine were doing the dishes, one washing, the other drying. I hid behind the door and watched the procession of pots and plates and silverware. Then I saw the cookie press. Swift pulled it dripping from the water and held it out to Maine, like an offering, and I knew great things would happen to me.

"Are Swift and Maine still alive?" I ask my father.

He puts the paper down. "Dana."

"I know, I know." We talked about that last night, too. One died before the other, he couldn't remember which.

Swift and Maine, where are you?

Come out from wherever you are, come out.

WHY WOULD A MAN

The week his divorce from Gail became final, Alex witnessed a fight between two Korean women; one bit off the tip of the other's little finger and swallowed it. Aside from the timing, there was no connection between the two events. He didn't even know the Koreans, had never met them before that night, that dinner party. But there he'd been with Maureen, an old friend from college. She knew the Koreans.

That day he'd been in Santa Cruz on business and had brought along Maureen's number in case he decided to look her up. Actually there were two numbers, which he'd copied from the address book at home, both written in Gail's hand; she'd been the one to keep up with Maureen in the eight years since college.

Alex called the first number from a pay phone. No answer. He dialed the second and got an acupuncture clinic. This time he asked for Maureen and heard, "Just a minute, please."

"Hello?" she said. "Alex!" While they talked, he pictured her as he'd last seen her, two years ago: the same as in college, the same flyaway hair and mismatched clothes — stripes with plaids, dots with stripes — clothes bought at rummage sales that somehow looked great on Maureen.

Her only really big news, she said, was that she had shortened her name to Maura and was studying to be an acupuncturist. Alex wondered if she knew about his big news, the divorce. Since she didn't mention Gail, he assumed she did, probably through Gail herself. In any case, he wasn't about to bring it up. Instead he told Maureen — Maura — about the business, his business, this business trip: he was down from Marin to drum up more customers, more restaurants. "I wholesale vegetables to restaurants … remember?"

"Oh, the weird vegetables, bok choy, baby this, baby that. Baby crookneck squash?"

"Right," he said, and when the conversation slowed, he asked her out to dinner.

"I'm supposed to have dinner at Dr. Kim's," she said. "Wait a second —"

Alex was put on hold. Who was Dr. Kim? He deposited another quarter, wishing he had phrased the invitation differently. It wasn't meant as a date; he just wanted to have dinner with an old friend. Ever since the divorce he'd been feeling nostalgic, lonesome, cut off. Divorced. The word was like cold steel, and he envisioned himself with a bad shave, ill-fitting clothes, frayed collars. But there was nothing wrong with his shave or his clothes. They weren't falling apart, certainly not his shirts, and Gail had never been the type to look after his clothes anyway. *He* felt frayed, that was it, as though his neck, his skin, could unravel like fabric.

"Alex?" He pressed the receiver to his ear more tightly. "You're invited too. Dinner at Dr. Kim's, how does that sound? I can give you directions here."

"Who is Dr. Kim?"

"What? Oh. This is her clinic." As though he ought to know. "Didn't I tell you? I'm studying here, under her supervision." Maura then gave him directions to the clinic, which he jotted down on the back of his motel receipt. Following an afternoon at restaurants — two French, one seafood, one health food — Alex headed over to the clinic. Maura's directions were needlessly complicated; he finally threw them aside and consulted a map.

The clinic was in a medical building. He gave his name to the receptionist and almost didn't recognize Maura when she passed by: white coat, rubber gloves, her flyaway hair cut short, smooth, parted on the side. She was carrying a tray of needles which, she explained, had just come out of the sterilizer. "Be right back," she said, and when she returned, minus the gloves and needles, they hugged each other. She offered to show him around the clinic.

"I can even give you a treatment," she said.

"For what?"

"Anything. Allergies, headaches, back trouble, nerves. Anything."

He passed on the treatment — he didn't like needles — but accepted the tour. While explaining the basics of acupuncture Maura showed him the sterilizer, the needles sorted by size. They peered into several examination rooms that didn't seem much different from any doctor's. Then she opened another door. Inside was a fat man lying on a table, stuck with needles like a pincushion. The needles were attached to wires, hooked up to a machine.

"What's he being treated for?" Alex whispered.

"Various things, obesity mostly." She closed the door.

"What about the machine? What's that do?"

She was about to answer when a tall Asian woman approached them in the hallway. "Dr. Kim," Maura said, touching her sleeve. "This is Alex."

Dr. Kim held out her hand and he shook it. "You're having dinner at my house," she said, and let his hand drop. Deliberately. Her eyes were dark and unreceptive. "Excuse me," she said and went into the fat man's room, closing the door.

Alex stared after her, insulted. Why had she acted that way? He turned to Maura — hadn't she noticed? She was describing how the machine warmed the needles, sent gentle waves of electricity throughout the body. "In the old days," she said, "they vibrated the needles by hand." Alex barely listened. The last thing he wanted was to have dinner at Dr. Kim's. But when he tried to figure a way out, some last-minute excuse, he felt exhausted, physically weak. In the past year he'd come to associate this feeling with Gail, to blame her for it. Before their separation he'd been cheerful and energetic enough, despite Gail's continual depressions, or maybe because of them. Then she'd moved out, leaving him with nothing but the furniture and a damp spirit. He couldn't help hating her for it even though he still, unfortunately, loved her.

Alex trailed after Maura without really seeing her, down the hallway, following only the heels of her shoes, the sound of her voice. She talked about Dr. Kim, how she was not only an acupuncturist but a medical doctor as well, how her parents had emigrated from Korea shortly after Dr. Kim was born.

"She was a genius as a child," Maura said, "a prodigy." Alex imagined Dr. Kim emerging from the womb a fully developed adult, complete with medical degrees.

Exchanging her white coat for a sweater, Maura said that Dr. Kim had taught her so much, *so much* about the workings of the body, the workings of the mind. "She's given me a sense of direction," she said, leading Alex out to the parking lot. He felt momentarily comforted by her baggy green sweater with its design of footballs across the back; this was the Maura, the Maureen he knew. She turned to face him. "Do you know what I mean?"

"Sort of."

Maura wanted to stop by her place to change, so Alex followed her there in his car. They parked in an alley and walked through a small courtyard littered with potted plants in various stages of decay.

"Those are my herbs, and that—" Maura pointed to a tiny, weed-infested plot—"that's my vegetable garden."

Alex glanced at the sliding glass doors of her apartment. A huge, hairy animal stood on its hind legs, licking the glass. "Is that a dog?"

"Dog? Oh, the dog. That's Mack. Do you grow vegetables?"

People always asked him that, assuming that since he sold vegetables, he grew them too. "No," he said. "No time or interest." He was working ten, twelve hours a day, and besides, why grow vegetables when he could have his pick from the warehouse? He wished Maura would hurry up and unlock the door. Her bug-eyed dog made him nervous; barking and howling, it pounded its paws on the glass as though any minute it might come crashing through. When finally she did open the door, the dog jumped up on Alex, paws on his shoulders, wagging, drooling, licking.

"Down!" Maura pulled the dog off. "He's been cooped up all day, I'd better walk him. You go on in."

Except for the futon mat on the floor, there was no place to sit, so Alex wandered around noticing the clothes in the bookcase and the books in the boxes. Typical Maureen. In college she had owned so many secondhand clothes she'd kept them in plastic bags under her bed, and she would be forever digging out some choice item to give you—a gold lamé scarf, black clumpy shoes from the fifties, a man's shirt with five species of birds all over it. "Here, take it," she'd say. Once, when she heard that he and Gail were thinking of getting married, she rummaged around and pulled out a gaudy satin wedding gown with a six-foot-long train. Both of them winced. As it turned out, they didn't get married for another six years. They lived together all that time, and when they did finally marry, it was only to separate a year later. In fact, the wedding-dress incident had marked the beginning of Gail's indecision about their marriage, about him. She was the most indecisive person he had ever known. Deciding what to do on any given day was almost more than she could handle, and he sometimes thought the first and only decision of her life had been to leave him.

Alex opened the refrigerator, hoping for a beer or soda or juice, and was confronted with a multitude of small paper bags. Looking inside one, he saw a white hunk of something. Old cheese? He wasn't about to smell it. The only drinkable item in the refrigerator was a yellow viscous liquid in an unmarked jar. He drank water instead, rinsing out the glass first.

Maura was still a lousy housekeeper, that much hadn't changed. There were dog hairs on the futon, dust balls in the corners. In that way, she and Gail were alike, although Gail wasn't filthy, just disorganized. Wherever she went, clutter followed. She would announce she was going to clean out a closet, and hours later he'd find her lost in a pile of clothes, books, papers, and boxes, vaguely reading letters, on the verge of tears. "I feel so overwhelmed," she'd say, her small white face tense and frightened, the face of a displaced child; he'd always loved that face. It was true that once Gail left, there was a lot less clutter — Alex had been the superior housekeeper — but now the house was falling apart in ways he'd never anticipated. The roof leaked, the floors had warped, and recently there'd been an invasion of mice. He could find the droppings but not the mice. Although he'd set traps everywhere, he had yet to catch a single mouse.

On Maura's wall were two posters: the human body, front and back, speckled with red dots. Examining the dots more closely, Alex saw they were connected by lines, like a map of a subway system.

"Pressure points," said Maura when she returned. That's where the body stored toxins, she explained. If not released through acupuncture or massage, they would build to unhealthy levels. "Toxins contaminate the body," she said, "and that's what makes us sick." To Alex the theory seemed absurd, as though the body were a kind of toxic waste dump.

Then, without warning, Maura said, "I'm sorry to hear about your divorce."

So she did know. Alex braced himself for yet another discussion of his personal life. What happened? How's Gail taking it? Do you still see each other? Any chance you'll get back together? Are you seeing anybody else? All the stupid, useless questions people asked. Relatives, friends, people he hardly knew. Sometimes they even said, "Don't feel you have to talk about it." But that was exactly what they wanted, for him to talk about it.

Before Maura could ask any questions, he asked her a few. Impersonal questions. How did she like living in Santa Cruz? Had she met a lot of people? How did she like her apartment? Would she stay here or move?

"Move," she said. "It's the dog, he needs more room. He's not a puppy anymore."

While Maura changed in the bathroom, Alex watched the dog as it roamed the courtyard, knocking over pots left and right, urinating on the vegetables. When she came out, he barely recognized her. Again. Except for the sweater with the footballs, she must have thrown away her wild, rummage-sale clothes. What she had on now was disappointing, almost depressing: some drab green outfit, matching blouse and pants, and those black rubber-soled Chinese shoes that everyone wore these days.

Maura locked the dog inside and they left. She drove too fast — up, down, around hills, along cracked paved roads with soft shoulders and muddy potholes. Although it hadn't rained, everything was dripping, green, soggy, wet. "They don't get a lot of sun back here," Maura said at the base of the steepest hill yet. She floored it, wheels spinning, mud flying: up a dirt road not much wider than a path, barely enough room for a car, so overgrown with trees it was like driving through a beaver's nest, the branches so low they scraped the roof of the car.

"Wait'll you see Dr. Kim's house," she said as they passed an apple orchard, then a clearing. "There's a view of the ocean, the hills, the valleys ... "

Alex didn't see the house at first. It was sunk into the side of a hill, and they had to walk down some stairs to get there. Maura went in without knocking and Alex followed, into the kitchen, where Dr. Kim stood between two other Orientals, a man and a woman. The woman was much shorter than Dr. Kim, with shiny clipped hair, and the man was somewhere between their heights. He had on a dark suit, white socks, and sandals. Introductions were made by Dr. Kim, who then led them into the living room. Alex didn't quite catch the names of the man and woman, and when he asked Maura to repeat them, she whispered instead, "He's Dr. Kim's ex-husband, and that's his wife. They're all good friends."

In the living room were two couches at a right angle, a coffee table, a large picture window, bare walls. On the table were five glasses of white wine and another bottle, newly opened. Alex sat next to Maura on one couch, while Dr. Kim and her ex-husband and his wife — whatever their names were — sat on the other. Alex considered asking Maura for their names again, but she seemed so engrossed in the conversation, some of which was in a foreign language, that he decided not to bother. Since nobody included him in the talk and he didn't speak Korean, assuming the language *was* Korean, Alex gazed out the window. The view was spectacular: dark hills rolling out to the distant ocean, a pink sky, the sunset. It almost hurt to look at the horizon, it was so red, like something inflamed.

Already the wine had gone to his head. He was tired, hungry, and he couldn't get situated on the couch. It was the type with a low back and too many pillows — you either slumped back among them or sat up like a board. Straightening up, Alex turned his attention back to the conversation, the English part at least, only to find himself staring at the little woman. Compared with Dr. Kim she was tiny, a toy woman, yet not delicate or sweet. She was perched on the edge of the couch like a brittle doll, her wine glass poised on a kneecap the size of a silver dollar. From what Alex could gather, she was some kind of teacher, while Mr. Kim — he couldn't help thinking of him as Mr. Kim — was apparently a lawyer. The two of them, along with Dr. Kim, seemed to be discussing their respective students, clients, and patients, though clearly Dr. Kim dominated the conversation. For some reason Alex was surprised to hear Dr. Kim talk in Korean, and surprised whenever the little woman or Mr. Kim spoke in English. Maura didn't say a word, only listened with a rapt expression. As if *she* could understand Korean. Alex was annoyed: since they could all speak English, why didn't they?

And the invitation had been for dinner, hadn't it? Or were they going to sit here all night drinking wine? He poured himself another glass, finishing off the bottle. Instantly Mr. Kim hopped up and went into the kitchen, returning with a new bottle which, strangely, he placed next to Alex. What was this, some kind of hint? Alex put his glass down and looked at Mr. Kim, who smiled back politely and stationed himself by the other couch.

All conversation had stopped, all faces turned to Dr. Kim. What were they waiting for? Alex noticed her charcoal gray suit, her long yet coarse fingers. At last she spoke to him, her dark eyes somehow deliberate, as deliberate as when she had dropped his hand earlier that day. "What is it that you do, Alex?"

"I'm a wholesaler," he said. "I sell vegetables to restaurants."

"Exotic vegetables," Maura added, as if that detail would make a difference. Surprisingly, it did. Everyone smiled, even Dr. Kim.

"Tell them," said Maura.

He started by listing the vegetables he sold. Bok choy, baby okra and artichokes, fiddlehead ferns, diakon sprouts, radicchio, certain varieties of mushrooms: oyster, shiitake, chanterelle . . . He had always liked talking about his vegetables. He felt an affection for their names, their odd shapes and sizes, their tastes. And he considered them superior to what most people thought of as vegetables — green beans, corn, carrots, iceberg lettuce, dull and ordinary. Next he described the mechanics of wholesaling: the delivery trucks, the early-morning phone calls, the farmers, the chefs. Before he knew it, he was explaining how he'd gotten into wholesaling vegetables in the first place. The summers in his father's markets, the double major in business and botany, the MBA, the stint at the L.A. Produce Market, the start-up funds and business loans. A distinct wave of drunkenness passed through him. Though he didn't slur his words, he felt dizzy, boozy, as if his organs had come unmoored. *Floating kidney.* The phrase dipped and swayed in his mind. Floating kidney. Wasn't that a disease? He paused, more than ready for someone to interrupt, ask a question, change the subject. But they all looked at him, waiting, expectant. He realized he was in the middle of a sentence, only he couldn't remember which sentence.

"Go on," Dr. Kim said.

"I forgot what I was — "

"You were talking about a loan."

"Oh." Reluctantly he picked up where he had left off: once he'd secured a loan, he moved the business out of his garage and into a dilapidated warehouse. He brought the story back around to the present, his current warehouse, the long hours, the risks involved, his plans to expand into supermarkets. Never had he talked so much about this one subject, his business. He wondered why he kept *on* talking; why couldn't he stop? He tried to read the faces of the others; weren't they bored yet? But their faces were blank. He noticed the hair of all three women, cut in exactly the same style—parted on the left, the hair no longer than their chins. The effect made him stop talking. He simply stopped.

"In short," said Dr. Kim, "you're a middleman. That's all you're really trying to say."

Alex leaned back against the pillows. Everything the woman said came out like an insult. "If you want to be simplistic about it, yes. I'm a middleman."

There was a long silence.

"Why?" Dr. Kim said.

"Why what?"

"Why do you do what you do?"

"I like it," he said. "I like to think of people—" He shifted on the couch. "I like to think of people sitting in restaurants, eating my vegetables."

"How humble," she said.

Alex glanced around at the others for a clue. What was going on here? Maura was absolutely no help. There she sat, head in hand, elbow on knee, gazing into space. And over by the couch stood Mr. Kim; in all this time he hadn't moved. As for his wife, the little woman, she merely tapped her tiny high-heeled shoe and sipped at her wine.

"Why would a man sell vegetables he doesn't grow?" said Dr. Kim. "You don't grow them, do you?"

"No. Am I supposed to?"

"Why would a man sell vegetables he doesn't grow?"

"I don't want to *grow* the vegetables, I want to sell them—"

"Exactly," she said.

"Exactly?" Alex looked again at the others. No one defended him, certainly not Maura, who acted as if Dr. Kim's question were wise indeed, one they would all do well to consider. "How do you think restaurants get their vegetables? Do you think the chefs go out and pick them by hand? I sell vegetables to restaurants, I provide a service. Do you have a problem with that?"

"I'm only asking a question," Dr. Kim said. "Why would a man sell vegetables he doesn't grow?"

"Why would a doctor, a woman, stick needles into people?"

Dr. Kim laughed, a laugh that indicated she thought it a clever, if irrelevant, question, one that needed no reply. "Really, you take my questions too seriously." And with that, Dr. Kim stood up.

Maura whispered to Alex, "She likes to invent questions."

"I don't think she likes to hear the answers," he said as Dr. Kim left the room, followed by Mr. Kim, who in turn was followed by the little woman.

"That means it's time to eat," Maura explained.

"What is this, a religious cult?"

He apologized immediately; Maura looked so hurt. And as they went into the kitchen, Alex thought about the way Dr. Kim's ex-husband had followed her out of the room. Soundless in his sandals, like a goddamn servant. He pitied the man for ever having been married to Dr. Kim. He could just imagine it, being put on trial for various minor offenses, day in, day out. "Yes," she would say, "but why would a man leave wet towels on a door when he could hang them on a towel rack?"

"Vegetables," Dr. Kim announced, pulling the lid from the steaming pot on the stove.

"She grows them herself," Maura told Alex.

"I figured." He could just picture the vegetables from her garden, like most homegrown vegetables: small, pale, bug-eaten, pathetic.

Serving up plates of brown rice and vegetables smothered in sauce, Dr. Kim passed them around as though to recipients in a soup line. Then they all marched out to the dining room. Dr. Kim presided over the meal while the others, aside from nipping at their wine now and then, huddled down to their plates, eating quickly, furtively. Not Alex. He sat across from Dr. Kim and deliberately picked at his food. The vegetables were ordinary, overcooked, and overwhelmed by Dr. Kim's phlegmlike cheese sauce. Then he tasted something delicious, unexpected: an oyster mushroom. He found another and held it up on his fork. "I suppose you grow these too?" he asked Dr. Kim.

"Here in this house, as a matter of fact," she said. "Most people think they're grown only outside, under trees. But you, of course, know better."

As she described in detail how she had converted one bathroom into a small mushroom farm, Alex wondered about the others. Surely they had heard all this before, though you'd never guess from the way Maura leaned forward in her chair, as if receiving divine knowledge. Mr. Kim was as passive as always, but when he caught Alex's eye, he smiled. It was like a reflex; whenever he looked at Alex, he smiled. Only the little woman appeared bored, dinging the side of her wine glass with her tiny, sharp, manicured nails. Then she shifted her eyes without moving her head, back and forth, between Dr. Kim and Alex, back and forth, like a cat.

"You claim to sell mushrooms," Dr. Kim was saying now. "But the mushroom is not a vegetable, it's a fungus of the class Basidiomycetes."

"I'm well aware of that," said Alex, though he hadn't known the exact name of the class. Did the woman have to be an expert on everything? Fortunately she didn't make an issue of it. Instead she rose from the table and invited Alex to see her mushrooms.

Leaving the others to clean up, Dr. Kim led him into another part of the house, past bedrooms and studies lined with books, to a dimly lit bathroom. In the tub and along the walls were shelves of mushrooms growing in trays of dirt or blocks of compressed sawdust. Alex waited for the lecture to begin, for Dr. Kim to tell him that mushrooms were a source of protein or prevented cancer, something along that line. But she hardly said a word other than to point out the two types she grew: the common mushroom found in any market and the oyster.

While she busied herself in the room, Alex examined her oyster mushrooms, admiring their curved stalks and creamy pearl gray caps, soft as eyelids. Of all the mushrooms he sold, the oyster was his favorite. It wasn't tough and meaty like the shiitake but tender, almost helplessly delicate. Alex was enjoying himself for the first time that night. He even felt a certain affinity with Dr. Kim, a feeling that she too liked this room with its moist, clammy odor, the smell that only mushrooms have, of things growing fast, faster than nature intended. He watched as she went from shelf to shelf, misting the mushrooms with water. Then she examined them individually, touching a cap or stalk here and there, as though checking cribs in a nursery.

"Look." She held out a block of tiny oyster mushrooms, their heads like pins. They had just begun to fruit but were shriveling around the edges. "Look," she said.

Alex saw the dark rot forming on the crust of the block and all at once experienced an ache, pity for these mushrooms that couldn't take care of themselves but depended on Dr. Kim for survival. Sensing her eyes on him, he felt compelled to ask, "How long have you been growing mushrooms?"

"A long time," she said, "a very long time."

The answer had a strange effect on him. It was all that an answer should be: sad and human, elegant and true. Also, the answer made him feel that Dr. Kim understood him and that up until now, he had misunderstood her. And in still another sense, the answer made him want to seek protection, though he couldn't say why.

In any case, when Dr. Kim suggested they join the others in the living room, Alex followed, docile and trusting. But when he actually saw the others — Mr. Kim and the little woman on one couch, Maura on the floor in front of them — he didn't know whether to trust Dr. Kim or not. Why should he, after the way she had acted all night?

Alex sat beside her. Exactly where she told him to sit, he noticed. She poured him a glass of wine and he drank it. She poured him another glass and he drank that too. He began to think he was in love with her. What was the matter with him anyway? He thought of the Wizard of Oz: "Are you a good witch or a bad witch?" That's what he wanted to know, was she good or bad?

He could certainly understand why Maura had fallen under her spell. The woman was charismatic, larger than life. He looked at her now, the way she monopolized the conversation with her voice, her hands, and how the others appeared to sway beneath the movements of her long, ringless fingers. He too was swaying. You're drunk, he told himself. There was something he wanted to tell Dr. Kim; he didn't know what. As if able to sense this, she turned to him, the pillows molding themselves around her like obedient pets. "Tell me about your wife," she said.

"Ex-wife." Not this, he didn't want to talk about this.

"Maura told me," she said.

"Told you what?"

"About your divorce."

He couldn't believe the woman's audacity, but what he really couldn't believe was that he was going to tell her all about it. And that in the end he would be grateful to her for getting this information out of him. He told her about the two incidents that bothered him most. The first had occurred the night before the wedding, at the rehearsal dinner. Getting to the dinner was bad enough. He'd come home from work to find Gail standing at the door naked, a mascara wand in her hand. "All afternoon I've been trying to put on makeup," she said. She was beautiful like that, naked, but a wreck. "I have to wear makeup, how can I not wear makeup? How can we get married? I don't even know how to put on makeup." Once he'd supervised the putting on of makeup and got her into her dress — she almost left the house without her slip, and the dress was see-through — they'd driven to the rehearsal dinner fighting all the way.

"About nothing," he told Dr. Kim. At the dinner Gail was so nervous that she went around telling everyone she might not show up the next day. They thought she was kidding, but no, she insisted she was perfectly serious. He would never forget the faces of his family, his friends. Confused, embarrassed. He felt they would never forgive him for being such a fool.

Here Alex paused, though Dr. Kim didn't ask questions. She listened. He mentioned, because he thought he should, that the wedding had gone fine, although both he and Gail looked like ghosts in the pictures. The other incident had happened six months ago, around the time the divorce papers were being drawn up. Gail had come over to discuss *something*, as she put it. Secretly he hoped for a reconciliation, but no, she had a list of things she wanted from the house, a couch in particular. He refused to give her the couch. She could have everything else, but not that. He loved that couch; it was covered in a peach-rose fabric. She threw a tantrum until, finally, he gave in. But when she got her way, instead of being pleased, she broke a bottle of wine on the floor—

Dr. Kim interrupted. "Did you tell her you loved her?"

"That night?"

"Any night."

"Of course," he said and went on with his story. What bothered him most, he told Dr. Kim, was the look of hatred on her face, especially when she broke the bottle. He had tried to give her everything before and during their marriage, and when she wanted a divorce, he gave her that too. The more he did for her, the more he tried to make her happy, the more she hated him. "People like me," he said, "can't make people like Gail happy."

"Did you tell her you loved her?"

"Why do you keep asking me that? Of course I told her I loved her; I did everything I knew how to do—"

"But did you tell her?"

"*Yes,* I told her. I told her and told her."

"Why would a man—"

"Don't ask me that—"

"Why would a man divorce a woman he loves?"

"Because she wanted it that way, all right?"

"But why would a—"

"Stop asking me questions! What are you, my analyst? First you want to know why I sell vegetables instead of grow them, or some stupid thing. Now you want to know—" He stood up. The others watched him, interested. "What *I* want to know is why do you want to know?"

Dr. Kim got up and started to leave the room. "Wait a minute," Alex said, "I want to ask you a question."

"Yes?"

"When I met you at the clinic today, why did you let go of my hand like that?"

"Because it was cold and white."

Alex sat down on the couch, his body heavy, sinking into the pillows. "Maura," said Dr. Kim, "why not give your friend a back rub?"

Maura hopped to her feet as if glad to be of service. To Dr. Kim, not Alex. Still, he allowed her to lead him over to a rug not far from the couches. She asked him to remove his shirt and lie on his stomach, and he complied, thinking of all the things he could say to her about Dr. Kim. The woman was a tyrant who enjoyed dissecting people's brains, it was as simple as that. And you're just her dumb little handmaiden, he wanted to tell Maura. But he was too worn out to say anything. Never had a back rub felt so soothing.

Then he heard tense, angry, foreign voices, the voices of Dr. Kim and the little woman. From where he lay, Alex could see them arguing on the couch with Mr. Kim between them. They leaned across him, almost growling, while Mr. Kim sat placidly as though listening to nothing more taxing than a difficult passage of music. And judging from the feel of Maura's hands on his back, she too was undisturbed. The voices settled into a low rumble for a while, then rose to a screeching.

"What are they fighting about?" said Alex, trying to get up despite Maura's sitting on his back.

"We're discussing vegetables," said Dr. Kim, to which the little woman added, "None of your business!"

"Shouldn't we leave?" Alex asked Maura.

"Dr. Kim likes me to stay."

"What's that supposed to mean? Is it always like this around here?"

She eased his shoulders back down onto the rug. "I have the greatest faith in Dr. Kim," she said and started the back rub all over again, going from his neck to his tailbone, concentrating on his shoulder blades. "Please try to relax," she said. That was the crazy thing: despite the racket, he did relax — his muscles simply gave up fighting. In time he even got used to the voices, the volume rising and falling; there was a certain music to it all. He began to doze, only to be awakened by Maura's fingers jabbing into his backbone as if she were trying to disconnect the vertebrae.

"What are you doing!"

"Pressure-point massage," she said. "It hurts because of the toxins."

It hurt like hell. What was in there that could cause so much pain? What were toxins anyway? He imagined the line of pressure points up and down his back, little bulbs filled to bursting, pus and words and bitterness. He heard a voice inside his head, a singsong voice he dreaded. Why would a man divorce a woman he loves? Because he doesn't really love her. No, no, too simple. It was more complicated than that. Too complicated. He listened to Dr. Kim and the little woman, their unintelligible words rising, falling, rising, the perfect background for his thoughts. Sometimes shrill, sometimes plaintive, their voices became figures in his mind, nasty Oriental nymphs, bleached white, bodies naked, yelping, screeching, howling, keening, all the sounds of love.

Dazed, he opened his eyes. The little woman was hurling a vase; it hit the wall and shattered. She screamed in the face of Dr. Kim, who yowled back in Korean, while the odd Mr. Kim remained on the couch, peering about like a bird. The little woman picked up something else to throw, a dish. Mr. Kim rose to his feet and gently removed it from her hands. He spoke soothing words to both women, then returned to the couch. The women embraced, and the little woman brought Dr. Kim's hand to her cheek, kissing the fingers.

The next thing Alex knew he was on his knees, searching for the tip of Dr. Kim's little finger. Everyone had rushed at the little woman, but she held fast with her teeth. And nobody knew that the little woman had actually swallowed the tip of Dr. Kim's little finger until she made a point of telling Alex, who continued to grope around on the floor, thinking perhaps she'd been mistaken.

Then Alex was speeding to the hospital in a car, holding on to Dr. Kim in the back seat while Maura drove. Dr. Kim's face was chalk white, and she had a kitchen towel wrapped around her finger, but she was talking, conjugating verbs in German, French, and Spanish. She said it felt better to talk. Actually she was in better shape than Alex. He couldn't stop thinking about the tip of Dr. Kim's little finger. You'd think it was his finger. Dr. Kim herself said it would be fine, all she needed was a few stitches. Alex had to keep reminding himself — it wasn't the whole finger, it wasn't half, or even a third, one-fourth, or one-eighth of Dr. Kim's little finger. It was probably less than one-sixteenth: a tiny bit of the nail, no bone loss, only the very, very tip. Still, he could not stop thinking about the tip of Dr. Kim's little finger. He felt attached to it somehow, even now as it lay in the pit of the little woman's stomach. He considered: if I'm attached to the tip of Dr. Kim's little finger and the tip of Dr. Kim's finger is inside the little woman's stomach, then I'm attached to the lining of that stomach. Circular logic, but he felt better, more connected to all living things.

WICKED

My stepsister is my older brother's ex-girlfriend. His name is Jonathan, and he and Mabe were girlfriend and boyfriend years ago in high school, long before my father married Margaret Ann. I suppose that's how Rex — my father — and Margaret Ann met: through their kids dating and going on car rallies. Anyway, they got married and we all went to Hawaii, on a trip. This was back in the days when Rex and Margaret Ann thought we'd all get along just great as a family, that we'd all *like* each other. I can see why they thought so — since Mabe and Jonathan used to go together and still liked each other as friends, and Mabe's brother was a little older than me, and then there was Vinny, my younger brother, and I don't know where he fit in, but there we were, in Hawaii. To back up: in the fall of that year my father married Margaret Ann, bringing to the new marriage us — Jonathan, twenty-one; me, fifteen; Vinny, thirteen.

Margaret Ann was a divorcee. She had two kids — Mabe, the same age as Jonathan, and Richard, sixteen.

All very convenient in Hawaii because Richard went off not with me but with Vinny, snorkeling, hiking, scuba diving, fishing. I don't know where Jonathan and Mabe went or what they did, but I was suspicious. Most of the time I wasn't invited along with either party, nor did I care to hang around with Rex and Margaret Ann, so I sat on the beach and put on baby oil and hoped some cute boy would talk to me. Sometimes I hitched into Lahaina and went to the Dairy Queen.

The trip to Hawaii was made more confusing by the fact it was Rex and Margaret Ann's honeymoon. They thought we'd like to tag along since, after all, we were family now.

■ Our condo was down the street from the big resort hotels, the Hilton and I can't remember the name of the other one, but both had golf courses and parklike grounds with frangipani trees, couples walking beneath them holding hands. Our condo was squeezed onto a spit of land between the street and the beach. It wasn't gracious, but utilitarian. The rooms — three rooms joined by doors — came equipped with kitchens that Margaret Ann expected us to cook in. Breakfast and lunch, that was the deal. She and Rex would take us out for dinner.

So the minute we got there Margaret Ann herded us back into the car for a trip to the market. "Here's twenty dollars," she said to each of us, pressing bills into our hands. "Make it last." We wandered around the market, aghast at the tourist prices — double what we would pay in California. Margaret Ann watched us, triumphant, as if to say: You see what it is to run a home? Margaret Ann thought housekeeping was on par with running the country: full of important lessons about morality and ingenuity and good old-fashioned common sense.

I had liked her better before my father married her. Way before, before they got engaged. Back then she used to take me shopping, and in some ways it was more fun than if my real mother had been around to take me; Margaret Ann had me try on clothes that would've shocked my mother, would've shocked *any* mother. She saw nothing wrong with miniskirts as long as your legs were good. "And yours are," she'd say, handing a skirt through the dressing-room curtain. Margaret Ann thought I was unique then, or maybe she was courting me the same way Rex was courting her. Once their engagement was assured, however, she treated me like an enemy warship to be monitored at all times. She thought I was spoiled, Rex said; he regularly reported to me what she thought of me: Margaret Ann thinks you should have been more grateful for the dinner she cooked last night. Margaret Ann thinks your table manners could use some improvement. Margaret Ann thinks you need a new bra.

"What, now she's inspecting my bosoms?" I was self-conscious enough. My breasts didn't appear to float as they were supposed to. They sagged, I thought. I was only fifteen and I, *they,* looked forty.

"She just wants to help," Rex said. "Who else is going to tell you?"

"You're telling me. For her. Why doesn't she talk to me about it if she's so concerned?"

He made another attempt, clearing his throat. "I — I think you're being unfair about Margaret Ann. She only wants the best for you. She knows about these things." What things, I used to wonder. They were never specified. "She has a lot of wisdom to impart, I think, and if you would only listen — "

"Oh shut up, Daddy," I said.

■ Mabe was nothing like her mother. She had a sense of humor, she was sensitive. She thought I had some intelligence and treated me accordingly.

Wicked, we used to call each other — for wicked stepsisters. At six feet, a full foot taller than me, Mabe smoked like a fiend, and in her presence, even at the age of fifteen in Hawaii, so did I. What pleasure it gave me, each of us reading in our beds late at night, the smoke in layers above us like smog, and she would ask me what I thought of this book, that book. She was destined to become a college professor; you could see it even then.

It fascinated me, trying to put this six-foot-tall, smoking, book-reading professor-to-be together with the person who went off with my brother in Hawaii, presumably to rekindle their high-school romance. She wore short-shorts — rather, her legs were just so long — and sandals made of strips of canvas. Her wild wavy hair was down then, not bundled up on top of her head as it was at night.

I wanted to be just like her.

But at fifteen I had a neck like a water heater. To my face Margaret Ann said I could be petite if only I'd lose a few pounds. Should be petite, her tone of voice hinted, as if it were my duty. Forget about my neck, my horse-sized hipbones, which jutted up and out so far I could not wear a bikini for fear you could see everything when I was lying down.

"Look at those bones," she'd said the week before the wedding, holding up my wrist and inspecting it. As if her impending marriage to my father gave her the right.

"Don't touch me," I said.

"What I wouldn't give for such teeny-tiny bones."

"Daddy!" I bleated.

"And those feet!" Margaret Ann wore size nine-and-a-half shoes, the one and only thing she'd change about herself in her next life, she said. "That's not bone on your hips, Frances, it's too much ice cream!"

Margaret Ann had never seen me in a bikini, but even if she had, my figure, my weight, was still her business. Was everybody's business: Vinny, two years younger than me yet wider and just as tall, the fat little tank, thought nothing of hoisting me over his shoulder and carrying me to a scale, just to see how I was doing in that department.

My real mother was as good as Margaret Ann was wicked. True, she'd deserted us when Vinny was a baby and I didn't even remember her, and my father had had her declared dead finally so he could remarry, but I knew she was good. Margaret Ann was wicked.

But back to Hawaii. Each night the seven of us sat at a big round dinner table loaded with pineapples stuffed with chicken and mahi-mahi, while Rex and Margaret Ann drank toasts to each other and loudly proclaimed to everybody in the restaurant that they were on their honeymoon.

"Well then, who might these people be?" our waiter would say, feigning wonderment — any idiot could see he'd heard their proclamations from across the room.

"Our children!" Rex and Margaret Ann answered in unison. "Ha, ha!"

They thought it a delightful joke, never considering for a moment it was at our expense. *You went on your parents' honeymoon?* We would have to live with this the rest of our lives.

■ My new brother, my stepbrother Richard, was something else. His hair combed back, the most perfect and enigmatic smile, he was like a foreign movie star without the accent. At first I was in love, though he was a little undeveloped for his age. Short was what it came down to. But you could see that someday he would be a knockout. "Frances," he said to me. "Now that we're related . . ."

"Yes, Richard?" Puckering up my lips for a kiss . . . no, that wasn't right! We were family now, forever connected by marriage.

"Now that we're related, will you do me a favor?"

The first few days in Hawaii I lugged his conch shells up the stairs so he could boil them; I dug out the insides after they were cooked. I lent him toothpaste. I retrieved his muddy sneakers from the car. I folded his clean white socks.

"Don't do that!" Mabe said. "He's a lazy bum. He's taking advantage of you."

"Oh, I don't mind," I said.

"You should." And off she went with Jonathan.

He and Richard and Vinny ("the boys," Margaret Ann called them) shared a room at the condo, and it was mile high with dirty clothes and booty from Richard's snorkeling and beachcombing and hiking expeditions: smelly old shells and dead fish he'd tried to cook via hangers over the burners marshmallow-style; the discarded horns of some mythical Hawaiian beast, Richard said; rock samples; coconuts, pineapples — very sour, not like the ones from the expensive market — and a so-called papaya ("This is a rotten apple, Richard," Mabe said); and wilted flowers Vinny kept trying to weave into leis with the hangers left over from the fish.

"Awful," Margaret Ann pronounced the room the one time she ventured into it, only to retreat to the unit she shared with Rex. Correction: Rex was trapped in there, which is why Mabe and I were forced to pass so many evenings in the boys' room. Our room was next to the newly wedded couple's, and they'd neglected to check the thickness of the walls before bringing us here on their honeymoon.

Every night it was *uhnnn, uhnnn,* OOOHHH, and Mabe would say, "Let's go next door, Wicked." Two, three hours we'd be stuck in there. "Can't we go to our room yet?" I'd ask Mabe, knowing it would be very, very late before we could return to our beds to lie on our backs and smoke cigarettes.

"I'll go see." A couple of seconds later, closing the door behind her: "No, Wicked."

I was always grateful she didn't use these opportunities to sneak off with Jonathan. Not that he'd go: at night Jonathan brooded in front of the TV, oblivious to her, to us, to the smell even of rancid fish and gardenias. Mabe had too much pride to hound him, so she ignored him, more and more pointedly as the honeymoon dragged on.

Really, we all got along very well, considering. The first few days anyway.

■ In one way I was glad Rex married Margaret Ann — maybe not her, but that he got married — because I liked acquiring more family. I felt safer somehow. And I liked referring to my stepsister, my stepbrother. "Oh, that's my stepbrother Richard," I might say to my friends. "Isn't he adorable?"

I didn't know how to refer to Margaret Ann. Saying "my stepmother" seemed too intimate, and I could never say it without sounding snide, as though I were slandering her rather than stating a fact.

M.A., I began calling her on the honeymoon, though never to her face. The Margaret part always made me think of the queen and her horsey sister, not an inaccurate comparison. All Margaret Ann needed was one of their hats.

If her liabilities were her feet and thighs, she said, her main asset was her waist. Personally I thought she should change herself over entirely, starting with her hairdo, which did resemble a kind of hat, layered and lacquered and woven together like acrylic.

To accentuate her waist she wore what she called her "little jackets." Short-waisted jackets that stopped exactly at, and drew attention to, her marvelous waistline. On the honeymoon I learned that Margaret Ann did windmills, her only form of exercise, and waist cinchers, where you put your hands on your hips and swivel like a searchlight. M.A. did this in pink fuzzy slippers, daily, before she took her daily bubble bath. Her bath was her form of meditation, she said, and she couldn't understand why people needed psychotherapy. Besides, Margaret Ann liked to say, bubble baths hardly cost anything. At this she would look pointedly at me.

Since age thirteen I'd been seeing a psychologist.

Psychologists, Margaret Ann said, were for people who didn't know themselves. Who had no respect for themselves. Who had no self-esteem. She'd pause here to allow for me to draw the necessary conclusion.

Other than the fact I had good legs, Margaret Ann seemed to find little about me worthwhile. Or as my father put it during the honeymoon on one of our walks—he would invite me to join him for a walk on the beach expressly for the purpose of telling me what Margaret Ann thought of me—"Margaret Ann thinks you don't like yourself."

"You mean *she* doesn't like me," I said.

He dropped that subject quickly enough. On to the next: "Margaret Ann thinks you ought to take secretarial courses."

"I'm not going to be a secretary, Daddy." Like Margaret Ann had been, I might've added, the one year of her life she'd worked. And she hadn't even been a secretary, but a receptionist.

"She thinks you don't have any skills. Drawing classes are nice, but—" He shriveled up his lips in distaste.

"Now you even look like her," I said.

"Who?"

"Margaret Ann."

"I'm afraid I don't understand."

"You look like Margaret Ann. Now that you're married to her, you look like her. Get it?"

"How about a typing class?" he said. "In case college doesn't work out."

"Why wouldn't college work out?" I slitted my eyes. What were he and M.A. up to?

"Well, let's just say it didn't. Even if it did, learning how to type would be a good idea."

"I'm going to college, Daddy."

"Of course you are! Margaret Ann just thinks that, well, when she was in college . . ." Margaret Ann's college days had ended some thirty years ago but were still a current subject between the two of them. "When I was in the Practice House," Margaret Ann would begin while my father stood there agog, his hand cupped to his slightly deaf ear so he wouldn't miss anything. Margaret Ann had been a Home Ec major. She talked about nutritious food preparation and the planning of meals, the proper sorting of laundry, her typing class of course (so she and her muffy friends could type their husbands' correspondence), not to mention the real baby she and her classmates had taken care of ("Now girls, this is the correct way to diaper"), the baby imported from somewhere. That's the part that always upset me — where did the baby come from? And when they finished playing house with it, where did the baby go? Where was its real mother? Margaret Ann never said.

"Please, Daddy, *please* don't tell me about when Margaret Ann was in college."

"All right, then," he said. "Margaret Ann thinks a modeling class might help."

"A what?"

"Modeling. Clothes, hair, makeup. Margaret Ann thinks it would help you develop poise."

The word made me think of two-fingered poi, the sweet white sticky stuff we'd been served at a luau the night before. "Why is it every time we're alone together you tell me what Margaret Ann thinks? What do you think?"

"Why do you dislike her?" He seemed so puzzled, so genuinely distraught that I felt sorry for him. All those years alone — twelve years without even a date — must've made him dotty.

"You really love her, don't you?" I said.

"Yes, yes, I do."

"I'll try," I said. "All right?" Anything to get that pathetic look off his face. "I'll try to like her. For you."

■ I met Roger on the beach. The first cute boy who ever talked to me of his own volition; who cared if he was a high school dropout? (M.A., that's who.)

"Do you want to go to the caves?" he asked me our fourth or fifth time together. Not dates. Roger wasn't into dates. He'd just ask me if I might happen to be on the beach the next day. If I happened to be there, he might happen to be there too, in his cutoffs and his shirt unbuttoned all the way.

"The caves? Cool." Being around Roger evoked such expressions from me — words I wouldn't use normally. "They're around here somewhere, right?" Nearby, I hoped, so I wouldn't have to ask Rex and Margaret Ann for permission.

"Twenty miles away."

"I might have to ask my father and M.A."

"Yeah?" A trace of disapproval in his voice? I was afraid he'd change his mind.

"Only twenty miles, huh?"

We drove there in a jeep belonging to his parents, who, I'd learned, lived here on the island. The caves were just off a beach, accessible only at lower tides. At high tide, Roger explained, the water didn't quite reach all the way back, making the caves good hiding places — nobody could wade in or out. He took my hand and guided me through a cave's opening, so narrow it was like threading ourselves through a needle. The tide rising now, water rushed and gurgled at our knees. "How long are we going to stay here?" I shouted.

"Till the tide's lower."

"How long's that?"

"How should I know? I've never been here before."

"But you said —"

"I never said I'd been here before." By now we'd reached wet sand, warm and soft as sinking into bread dough. The cave's opening was a bright blue hole surrounded by black, yet there was light coming from somewhere. I looked up. A natural skylight sculpted in lava.

"I've just heard about this place," Roger said and motioned me to sit beside him. "I wanted to see for myself. So here we are." He dug a joint out of his pocket. "Want some?"

"Sure." I'd only smoked twice before, both times getting so high I'd laughed hysterically, then panicked and cried. He handed the joint to me and I barely touched it to my lips.

"You're supposed to inhale it," he said.

"I know. I am." Here, away from my family, I felt suddenly much younger, as though Roger and I were playmates on an adventure in somebody's backyard. About to show each other our scrapes and bruises rather than about to kiss.

"Are you scared?" he said.

"My parents don't like you, you know." Parents? I'd never called them that before, and why was I talking about them anyway? Finally free of my family, and they were all I could think about. How Richard and Vinny would love this cave. Wondering if Mabe and Jonathan had been here, removed their clothing; I imagined Jonathan folding his swim trunks so they wouldn't get mussed. My mind settled on a detail of Margaret Ann's dress from the night before, the waistband. A cummer-bund, she'd called it.

Roger and I made love. My first time. We scarcely kissed or talked, and it seemed to me all I heard was embarrassed breathing, his and mine, and the rasping of sand on skin. It wasn't great or terrible, though I pretended it was marvelous. I actually used that word to Roger, and it was Margaret Ann's dull red lips I saw moving as though she were speaking.

That night at dinner we had roast pig. I couldn't eat it. Everyone's faces were that awful shiny pink that passes for a tan, even Margaret Ann's, despite her concoctions of hats and scarves.

"The last time we had pig," Margaret Ann said, "back on the mainland, that is. Rex? Do you remember?" She fiddled with the lei around her neck.

Rex cupped a hand to his ear. "Yes! Pig!"

"It was fresh roasted, like this one. Delicious! The marinade they used was made with peanut butter of all things. Indonesian, I believe."

"Delicious!" Rex said.

I pictured a sow in a yellow paper skirt. "I think I'm still high," I said under my breath, to myself. Not that anyone could hear me, down at the other end of the table from M.A. and Rex. "Pig. I'm afraid I'll get sick if they keep talking about pigs."

Richard nudged me. "This might surprise you," he whispered, "but I can't stand her. Even when I was a child. Can you imagine growing up with her as your mother? I never went to the school nurse. I was afraid they'd call her and she'd come get me."

"What would be so bad about that?"

"The others would see her coming down the hallway. They'd know she was my mother."

I uncrossed my legs; I was still in a lot of pain. I wanted to ask someone when it would go away. Mabe and Jonathan mechanically ate their dinners, buffered by Vinny, who played with his garnishes, putting a hat of pineapple on a crab apple, while Margaret Ann described and described and described all the pig she'd eaten, cooked so many ways.

"Mabe doesn't mind her," Richard said. "She puts up with her. I can't figure out how."

"Well, Mabel?" M.A. was off pigs and onto the quiz portion of dinner, in which she asked how we'd amused ourselves that day. *How we'd spent their honeymoon* was the way she always put it.

"I read on the beach," Mabe said.

"Jonathan?"

"I had a headache."

I knew very well he'd watched Mabe read from the condo's balcony, hidden behind a beach towel. Like he did every day. Now that she wouldn't have anything to do with him, he was gone on her.

"Richard?"

"Vinny and I caught a fish with our hands."

"Sure, Richard," Mabe said. "What was it, dead?"

"I had sexual intercourse today," I volunteered. "It was marvelous."

■ "Just kidding," I said a moment later. Margaret Ann was eyeing my father: I would be sure to hear about this tomorrow from him, how I'd once again ruined a perfectly lovely evening. On their honeymoon, no less.

Naturally, the following morning my father invited me to walk with him on the beach.

"Even if it isn't true . . . " he said. "Is it, Frances? Did you really?"

"Have sex? Of course not. A silly joke and Margaret Ann blows it all out of proportion." By now I almost believed myself that I hadn't. Not me, not Frances the Bookworm, not Frances who'd never had a boyfriend before, who'd never gone on a date. I felt thrilled, like I'd been soaking in a bathtub of gin, a woman now, a party girl, a rebel, wicked at last.

"Margaret Ann thinks — "

"Who cares what she thinks."

"Margaret Ann thinks you're sneaking around with that boy. Are you?"

"No! Why do you listen to her trashy talk?" Actually, Roger and I had plans to meet later that day at his parents' house — they'd be out — an event I both anticipated and dreaded. "She's always running me into the ground. I don't have to take this, you know." And I stormed off leaving my father to call and call my name.

■ The night before, once we were on our beds talking and smoking cigarettes, I'd said to Mabe, "I really did, Mabe. I had sex today."

"That was foolish."

It wasn't the response I'd expected.

"Did you use birth control?" she continued. "I suppose not. What if you get pregnant, Wicked, what're you going to do then?"

"You sound like your mother," I said.

"No, Mother doesn't think girls should have sex till they're married."

"But . . . " I couldn't explain what I meant. I had thought we might talk of love, that we might even giggle. My experience would be shared, then, with somebody, if not with Roger. Mabe was being so sensible.

After she turned off the light I whispered, "Does it have to hurt so much? Does it always hurt so much?"

"Sex stops hurting," she said. "The pain doesn't. Next time, Frances, be more careful. They sell condoms at the market, you know. Right next to the macadamia nuts."

■ I couldn't get rid of Richard the afternoon I was supposed to go to Roger's. He trailed me up and down the beach, revealing all. "You know what she did once? Get this, this is incredible. I asked where Mabe was and she told me she'd flushed her down the toilet. I was three. I believed her."

Now that I'd become his confidante, Richard had lost his appeal. He was whiny and boring, and seen through his eyes, Margaret Ann didn't seem so bad, just another weird, oppressive mother, like all my friends' mothers.

"Richard," I said, trying to change the subject, "do you have a girlfriend?"

"I don't have any friends, much less a girlfriend. She screwed me up, I'm telling you."

"But you're good looking, Richard. I'm sure a lot of girls are interested in you. I know my friends would be."

"You think so? Naw. . . Another thing she did? I must've been about ten. She took me out to buy me a jockstrap. My mother! My father should've done it — they were still married then — but she wouldn't let him."

"Listen, Richard, I hate to interrupt, but I have to go somewhere."

"Mind if I go with? I'm not doing anything."

"I have to go alone," I said. "It's a kind of date. Don't tell anyone, okay?"

He looked disappointed. "Okay," he said.

I left Richard on the road to Lahaina and hitched three miles to the crossroad Roger had told me about. From there I walked to the development, half a mile away. By the time I got to Roger's house, I'd convinced myself I was in love with him. Why else would I be doing this? Maybe today would be different. He'd greet me at the door with lover's words; he'd be wearing a smoking jacket — ridiculous, but that's what came to mind; we'd sip wine, perhaps. Beer at least. By the time I came to his driveway, I hung back. I wanted to savor my fantasy of how it would be, but instead I was assaulted by memories of how it had been yesterday: Roger's cut-off jeans, the fact he hadn't worn underwear, his bleary eyes, the awkward silences. What was I doing here? The guy was inarticulate, he didn't even know how to kiss.

I rang the doorbell. I never made it inside.

■ Later I wondered why I hadn't noticed Rex and Margaret Ann's car following me. Maybe because it was a rental car, not our Oldsmobile from home, or maybe secretly I'd wanted them to catch me.

"You're here to be with that boy," my father said.

"What of it?" I waited for Roger to join us in the driveway; he didn't, of course, the coward, if he was home at all.

"You lied to me," my father said. Behind him Margaret Ann fumed, her lips purplish. Actually, I thought she looked a little self-satisfied and pleased.

"I wouldn't have to lie if I could tell you the truth."

"You ruined Margaret Ann's honeymoon."

"I don't give a shit about Margaret Ann."

Her lips just got more bunched up, more purple.

"Frances," my father said, "I want you to apologize."

"For what?"

"For saying that word."

"Shit?" I almost laughed. "I'll say it again. Shit."

She was standing up so straight I thought she might creak if I touched her. Not that I would.

"You are the lie here, Margaret Ann. Playing up to me until you hooked my father, now you want to gyp me out of a college education and God knows what else."

In the movies the father is supposed to slap his forehead and say, You're right, by gum! This woman is an imposter! Get my lawyer on the phone, I want a divorce! Instead my father said, "All this — this — *language* just because Margaret Ann thinks you ought to take a typing course, Frances? Aren't you being a little unfair?"

"It's not only that, Daddy, it's everything."

"Such as?"

I didn't know how to begin. "You're always telling me what she thinks. I need a new bra. My table manners are atrocious. She thinks I'm fat. She thinks I'm crazy because I see a psychologist instead of taking bubble baths like her." It all sounded so trivial and insubstantial; how to describe the horror of Margaret Ann?

"I think you should apologize," my father said to me. Margaret Ann stood like a monument, her hair, her face, her hands, her size nine-and-a-half feet, stony and implacable.

"If anyone should apologize," I said, "she should."

"May I ask why?" my father said.

"She could've been someone to me, someone important — " I turned to Margaret Ann, pleading, "Remember when you used to take me shopping? You bought me miniskirts, you said I had good legs. You thought I was special then."

"So I did." Margaret Ann smiled, not exactly a pleasant smile, but I relaxed. Something good might come of this yet. "Your daughter," she then said to Rex, "is the most manipulative, callous person I have ever encountered. I've never known such ugliness to come from a child."

With that, she made her way back to the car, hurrying and stumbling in the open-toed pumps she believed made her feet appear smaller. My father gave me a despairing look, not of compassion but of extreme disappointment. I had let him down, not the other way around. He followed his wife, and I followed them both, pounding and pounding on the car's windows until my father rolled one down an inch.

"Tell Margaret Ann," I said, "that her own son hates her. It's all he talks about, how he hates his mother. Another thing: do you know the walls in your room are too thin? Every night we have to listen to you."

Halfway down the street, I looked back and saw my father comforting Margaret Ann behind the car's tinted windows. I imagined his arms encircling her waist, consoling that narrowest part of her.

■ Telling off Margaret Ann and the consequences—knowing I would be sent home early from the honeymoon, on the next plane—didn't seem so urgent when we found Jonathan on the roof of the condo threatening to jump. For Mabe, he shouted. For love. Stripped to his swim trunks, he crouched by the rain gutter, prepared to somersault over the edge.

"Love?" Mabe called up to him. "You don't love me, Jonathan. You don't. That's not what this is about."

"Don't argue with him," I said.

"Love!" my brother shouted. "For love!"

The police were here by now, and all the hotel guests, including Richard and Vinny, who hollered along with everyone else for Jonathan to hold on, don't jump. People we didn't even know, saying my brother's name and telling him *they* loved him, never mind who was breaking his heart. Rex and Margaret Ann—where had they been all this time, anyway?—pulled up in their car then. Rex got out, shading his eyes with his hand as if glimpsing a rare bird or a low-flying plane. "Dad!" I yelled as he and the police found each other in the crowd. "It's Jonathan, Dad. Do something!"

Mabe lit a cigarette, kept on trying. "This doesn't have anything to do with me, Jonathan! You're having a reaction. It's okay, but it's time to come down now. Come down!"

"A reaction to what?" I said.

"He asked me to marry him."

"Tell him you will. Tell him you love him."

"That would be a lie, Wicked. I can't do that." I saw her mother in her just then, that same principled, rigid, impractical morality.

"Love, love!" my brother screamed. "Love!" His voice hoarse, more like a squawk. "Love! Love!"

My father was climbing the stairs of the condo now. Oh no, the police were sending him up there, a terrible idea. He'd fidget, speak in platitudes: things will look brighter in the morning after a good night's sleep, son, you have your whole life ahead of you — comments that would make Jonathan jump for sure. I thought of creeping up there myself, comforting him, apologizing for my role in this. The morning of the wedding I'd goaded him into talking about our real mother, something he was always loath to do. "You don't remember even one little detail? You were seven when she left. How can you not remember?"

Jonathan had been knotting his tie. "All right," he said. "Here's one thing I remember."

I held my breath. This was it, I was sure, the memory, the detail that would explain everything. "She had this pin. Of a daisy. She wore it on her blouse sometimes, and when she hugged me, the pin would dig into my face."

I waited for him to go on. "So what happened?"

"That's it," he said, "that's the memory," and all during the wedding ceremony it was Jonathan I watched, not Rex or Margaret Ann, not the minister. It was Jonathan who held the rings, his face I'd watched for signs of sorrow.

"Love! Love, love!"

"Jonathan!" I begged. "Come down. Please!"

Another voice drowned mine out. "Stop this nonsense right now, Jonathan. You should be ashamed!" Margaret Ann. Right beside me, she was flapping something from her purse. "I have a picture of you here. You and Mabe at the senior prom." I knew that picture, the two of them looking anything but romantic, Jonathan in a dark suit — he'd refused to wear a tux — Mabe in pink organza, a dress sewn by her mother, I knew, Mabe's bare arms larger and stronger than Jonathan's could ever be. "You were a child then, practically a baby, but whatever you do, your father will have to look at this picture for the rest of his life, and others like it, and be reminded of this day."

Mabe tore the picture from her mother's fingers, crumpling it. "Of all pictures, Mother, this is the worst you could show him." Then to Jonathan, "Don't listen to her!"

He dove from the roof.

He landed in my shadow, virtually at my feet; perhaps he'd been aiming for Mabe. I heard the crack of bones, watched his horrifying skid before me, then he was unconscious.

His legs shattered, but he was otherwise unharmed. No broken neck or back, no paraplegia—a limp for the rest of his life, is all. He wasn't even committed, his jump being a kind of release. So he insisted. The day after on my takeoff from Maui, as I traced the plane's shadow over the ocean, I kept seeing again and again my brother's flight. Arms out, wavering like a bat, weighted down finally by his lower half: as if jumping off the high dive at the pool where we used to swim as kids.

■ It was Richard who died, several years later in a mountaineering accident. He'd been climbing without a rope. Before mountaineering it was kayaking, and before that, motorcycle racing: only dangerous sports would do. He had to get away from Margaret Ann, I think, turn himself inside out, or so it seemed to me when I went to watch him in a kayaking competition once. He refused to wear a helmet—it ruined the sport for him, he said—and each time the kayak rolled over, he reappeared grinning with blood on his face.

A year after Richard died, Margaret Ann divorced my father, saying she'd had enough of love, she wanted to be left alone. The odd thing is, she and I have developed a friendship of sorts, patched together by talk of clothes, trips, recipes: a phone relationship mostly. She advises me on men. *Don't let him rush you, marriage can be heartbreaking. Men are clumsy when it comes to comfort.* Her waistline continues to be small and marvelous, her feet square and wide as shoe boxes; sometimes I think they're growing as the rest of her shrinks.

The love between mother and child, she says, that's what endures. But she won't speak Richard's name or discuss the never-resolved bitterness between them. I can't tell if she is angry or sad or how she feels about where love leads. Once she loved Richard's father, then my father, who once upon a time loved my mother, who now loves someone else, or perhaps has other children. Or perhaps she's dead too. Love, I tell Margaret Ann, looks to me as black and life-giving as a swamp, there to nourish the generations or there to drown you. You don't get to choose; you can't predict. Still I can't help my slide into it, just as Richard's feet must've slipped sometimes on rock.

BREATHE SOMETHING NICE

WANDA

Pretty hair, the other girls told Wanda, as if it were the only thing about her worth mentioning. And a lie at that. It was like a sheep's, a wooly cap. Every Wednesday morning — and this Wanda lied to herself about — she dressed up to go to the Youth Authority, where she and the other girls were fulfilling their college's requirement for community service. Nothing too fancy or obvious, so the other girls wouldn't notice: a skirt or a print blouse, a bit of makeup. To cheer the guys up, she told herself, in case anybody ever asked. Helena in particular, whom she considered her best friend.

Wednesdays, Helena dressed down. Her combat clothes, she called them, baggy jeans, a men's Pendleton shirt, work boots — clothes she never wore otherwise. She was truly pretty, and every weekend Wanda tried to imagine what it was like being her, going to a concert or a movie, her long blond hair spilling carelessly over the collar of her coat.

Helena wasn't vain. That was just it; she was so natural, so unconscious of her beauty, so strong and unafraid, tough-talking yet nice.

But Wanda — "You're not nice, are you?" he'd said. Such green eyes, they made her own eyes water. "You're maybe like dirty inside, right?"

The first time he even talked to her he began saying those things; she could see that. "You know those trees outside?" he said. The winter trees in the distance, outside the Youth Authority, like crooked brooms. "That's how you are, inside. There." He stopped just short of touching her blouse, the place where her heart would be.

His name was Mace, John Mace, but she didn't know his first name was John until long after. All the guys called each other by their last names, Hey Mosely, Hey Swan, so she thought his name was Mace.

She liked that, Mace. The same as the small canister she carried in her pocket everywhere except here, because she wasn't allowed to bring it in, but she started bringing it anyway because he told her to. "I want to see it," he said. "I want to see you posing with it."

She saw herself with the mace between her legs, naked, then felt immediately ashamed and confused. That's not what he meant.

She'd had sex before, that wasn't it. She wasn't a virgin. None of the girls she admitted this to could believe it, especially Helena. "You? Wanda?" Helena had slept with only two or three guys (three if you counted everything but); Wanda wouldn't say exactly how many she'd slept with. The truth was she couldn't remember. It had started when she was fourteen, one afternoon with the guy next door, who was nineteen. She hadn't wanted to, not that he'd raped her exactly.

That night she'd sat down to dinner with her father, mother, brother, almost thinking that when they passed her the green beans she'd leave smudged fingerprints on the serving dish.

Little bitch, her father said when he found out. She'd told him because ... she still didn't know why. Maybe she thought he'd save her, harm the boy. Tell the parents at least, not yell at her in front of everybody at the dinner table.

From there things just happened, not right away but here and there, mistakes, accidents at first, then more deliberately, like a person on a diet meaning to do an errand and stopping off for ice cream afterward, knowing all along she would. Wanda didn't look the type to sleep with guys, anybody could see that. She was more the church type, first the Presbyterian church of her childhood and now the black Baptist church right off campus, where they sang and carried on around her, her in her old Sunday-school hat. The place was so forgiving and peaceful somehow, the room warm as bread, salty, smelling of people, and although no one touched her — an oddity, the only white person there — she felt enfolded in their arms.

The church type, but just last weekend she had let it happen again. She'd gone to a movie, lonely, and some guy with longish hair and wire-rimmed glasses (not the kind to screw around, she remembered thinking, too serious) had talked to her afterwards, suggesting they go out for coffee, but they wound up in his room smoking dope and fucking. Fucking. The inside of her soul once you peeled away the top layer.

"Hey," he said, "you're good," and she got dressed, never bothering to learn his name, lying about her own.

She had put on her raincoat, the kind secretaries wear to jobs at insurance agencies, and walked out the door. He didn't try to stop her.

HELENA

Marsanne, Natalie, Jan, all of us hated working at the Youth Authority. Wanda too — or so I thought at first. The drive itself was enough, five bucks of gas, for which we weren't reimbursed. "Think of it as a donation," the professor said. Which is why we had to carpool. So every Wednesday morning at 8:00, or 8:05 or 8:10, after delaying as long as we could, we floored it to the Youth Authority, south of town, south of South Stockton even, where guys eighteen, nineteen, twenty years old were locked up for all manner of offenses. Too young for a real jail, or as one of the inmates put it to me my first day there, "Too good, baby, you know what I mean."

We could've worked at the courthouse, we could've worked for the Senior Center or Meals on Wheels, had we known. But the professor had suggested it to each of us individually, how the Youth Authority needed folks — like you, he said earnestly — to tutor the inmates. The kids, he called them.

Remedial reading at the Youth Authority. Except the inmates never did any reading. They played checkers and talked. Made comments. Asked if we had boyfriends, what we did with our boyfriends. What we let our boyfriends do to us.

They talked about what they did to get themselves here. Robbed a store, sold drugs to the wrong guy. Knifed somebody. Lit a kid on a bicycle on fire. "You did not," I said to one of them once. "You just like to talk. You think I'm scared or impressed or something."

"That's right," he said, running his hand up and down the inside of his thigh. Laughing, half his teeth gone.

There was no supervision. An unarmed guard walked the corridors and sometimes poked his head in. Nobody to hear what they said to us, or did.

"Look," one of us would say every so often, "so you want to talk about this book?"

There were only five or six books, no other reading materials. "You bring in some magazines, you girls, know what I mean? The kind we don't got. Then we'll do some reading," an inmate would say while the others hooted and spit in their hands, his arm around the back of an empty chair as though feeling up a girl at the movies.

WANDA

John Mace wore white T-shirts, only white, Wanda noticed, although they could wear any color they liked, if they could get it.

He had perfectly manicured fingernails, for which he had her bring orange sticks and nail files. He showed her how to do her own nails; she'd never known before. "You push back the cuticles like this," he said. "You try it." She got so nervous with him watching her that she ripped into her own cuticle. "Gently," he said. "Hey, gently."

Within two months of going to the Youth Authority she had stopped even the pretense of talking to the other guys; John asked her please not to. "You're mine," he said, skimming the orange stick across the backs of her hands, tickling. "Anyway, they're trash, too rotten for you."

She hadn't forgotten what he'd first said to her, about being dirty, the trees.

"That nonsense," he said when she finally got up the courage to ask him. "I was just trying to make you mad. Because I'm here and you're there. Outside."

He wouldn't tell her what he'd done.

"Did you rob a store?"

"No."

"A gas station?"

"No."

"Deal drugs?"

"No."

She took a deep breath. "Did you hurt somebody?"

"Me? No."

He did tell her about his childhood. Father gambled, mother drank. So poor they used bath towels for curtains. One dead baby sister — he wouldn't tell her what she'd died of.

Wanda didn't question him further, though she wondered. He sounded too educated, and the details seemed out of a movie. Still his childhood, real or imagined, made her pity and love him all the more. Sometimes she would pace her room, list the deprivations and weep: the beatings, popcorn for dinner, spoiled Christmases, forgotten birthdays.

He asked her about the house she grew up in, the neighborhood, her friends, school, what she carried in her lunch box. "Did you have a swimming pool?"

"*My* parents? No."

"I thought you were rich." He seemed disappointed.

"Where did you get that idea?"

"Oh," he waved his hand. "We think all you girls are rich."

Helena said she thought it possible that John loved Wanda, although those weren't her exact words. "He loves your goodness," she told Wanda, "your sweetness, your charity."

Her charity. She had nothing but that to give; she couldn't sleep with him. Rather, he couldn't sleep with her. And if he could, what then? He'd just turned nineteen, a year younger than her, and what's more, he wouldn't get out until he was twenty-one. Not that he'd said anything about the future, their future. Yet Wanda actually saw herself—she confessed this much to Helena—as though in a fairy tale illustration: princess in a conical hat, silk or netting foaming out the top, cascading down her back like a ponytail (she used to try for the same effect as a child, a beach towel on her head). Yes, she had just the hair, the face, certainly the lips—tiny sweetheart rose lips. Yes, she and Helena had giggled together one night, high on a joint somebody had given them; yes, there was something tragically romantic about her. About Wanda, they said, as if discussing another girl.

He didn't like her name, that much he admitted. "Is it short for something?"

"No." She hung her head, afraid for a moment she would cry. "I can't help it, John."

John. Whenever she said his name aloud it sounded like food to her, a dessert a married couple might share on a small round table, their feet touching.

HELENA

I tried getting between them, pulling up a chair once. "What are you talking about?" I said. Mace just looked at me, those dead green eyes, and Wanda acted insecure, as though she thought I might steal him away. Then Mace kicked the chair, the chair I was about to sit in. "We're busy, can't you see that?" he said, and Wanda kind of moaned. "I'm sorry, Helena, you know how he is." As if she'd been married to the guy for years and couldn't be held responsible.

So I gave up on that plan and Wednesday mornings I spent just trying to survive. Most of all I hated the laughter. You'd be playing checkers, jumping a king or doing a double jump, and those guys would burst out laughing. For no reason. "What's so funny?" I'd say.

Or else they'd launch into their knives-guts-broken-bones rap about what somebody's going to do to somebody else when they get out. "I'm gonna get me a baseball bat and slam that sucker, his brains gonna be all over his mother's kitchen wall." That really got them laughing—stories of revenge.

He was different from the others, I'll grant that. He wouldn't stoop to such gore—it might dirty his T-shirt—and he talked like he'd at least gone to high school, which was more than you could say about the rest of them. But if I had to be stuck in a drainpipe with one of these guys, it'd be any one of them and not him. They're all talk, and it's the way he didn't talk that bothered me. He only talked about what he wanted you to know and headed off any questions he didn't want to answer. Such as how he wound up at the Youth Authority. "But don't you think you need to know that?" I told Wanda.

"He won't tell me."

As if that was that. I'd never met anyone as sweet and helpless and naive as Wanda. It used to drive me crazy. I'd try to get her mad, at him, at me, at anyone, anything. "I can't, Helena," she would say. "I guess I'm not a very angry person."

Everybody's angry, I told her.

I tried to get us out of going there. I made Wanda come with me to see the professor who got us into this situation. I had to do all the talking, naturally, since Wanda doesn't like to offend anybody and besides, she wanted to continue on at the Youth Authority so she could see *him.* She only pretended to hate it. I told the professor all about it, the lack of books, the lack of supervision, the talk we were subjected to. He listened patiently, almost mournfully, as though he understood my feelings perfectly. Then he said, "That's why this is such a vital experience for you, Helena. You too, Wanda. You won't get this kind of education anywhere else in this university." Then he explained to us all about the system—how we're all prisoners of the system, they're just on the inside and we're on the outside, it's all polarities, the same ball of wax, a society built on patriarchal authority. "Helena," he said at last, "don't you know it's impossible for you to drop this course? You'd lose three credits, you'd lose your scholarship, simple as that."

"Right," I said, standing up to leave. I grabbed Wanda's arm and tugged her after me like a rubber duck on a string. "Can you believe that guy?" I said in the hallway.

She blushed, and I knew it wasn't the professor she was thinking about.

So it was back to the Youth Authority. The next day, Wednesday, the guys there wanted to know what was the red stuff on my hand. Actually it was all up and down my arms and across my back, but I wasn't going to tell them that—they'd ask to see. "Poison oak," I said. "Got it hiking last weekend." Really I'd been fooling around with my boyfriend on a mountainside, and now I itched all over.

"I know a way you get rid of that," this guy named Roberto said. He was a big dumb guy, gentler than the others, just got quiet whenever they started their blood-and-gore talk. "You put a corn plaster on it."

"No, man, that takes too long. You want to get rid of it quick?" This was another guy, Fargo, he was the best at home remedies. "Bleach, man. Clorox bleach. Dilute it with water and pour it right on there." He snapped his fingers. "Next day, gone. You thank Fargo."

"What's he doing here?" I said, jerking my head in Mace's direction on the other side of the room, where he was holding court as always with only Wanda in attendance.

"Waiting to turn twenty-one, same as everybody else," Fargo said.

"I mean, what did he do to get here?"

"You like him?"

"No."

"You like us better." Big smile on Fargo's face, on all their faces.

"Not really," I said.

"Aw, girlie."

They never called us by our names. On the other hand, I'm not sure I wanted them knowing my name. "What did Mace do to get here?"

"Don't know," Fargo said. "Even if I did, I wouldn't tell. That's his business."

"Must be pretty bad," I said. Usually they were more than glad to fill you in, half of it lies maybe, although they never spoke for each other, only for themselves. Inmates' code of conduct, according to the professor. "Did he kill somebody?"

"That ain't true," one of them said. I already knew that—the murderers and rapists were in another building. I was just trying to goad them into telling me.

"Don't talk to her," Fargo said. So they didn't, and it was time to go anyway, down the hallway, led by a guard we hardly saw otherwise, out the gatehouse where this grandmother-type in a print dress always sat behind a desk and wished us a lovely week.

"What'd you talk to lover boy about?" I asked Wanda on the way home. I was getting nasty like that those last few weeks, digging at her with questions and so forth—trying to get her to see. "What stories did he tell you this time, Wanda?" It was her turn to drive and my question caused her to swerve. The other girls tittered. She wouldn't answer me and finally I thought I'd done it, gotten her mad. I rubbed my poor blistering back on the car seat like a snake molting its skin. "Did you find out what he did yet?" I said. "I wonder if the old lady at the front desk knows, I wonder if she'd tell. Or does she subscribe to the inmates' code of conduct?" I imagined her placing a shriveled finger to her lips, Sh-sh-sh.

"Helena," Wanda said at the next stoplight. Clearing her throat a little first. Her soft white hands squirmed on the steering wheel. "Helena? I wish you wouldn't."

That's Wanda losing her temper. As mad as I ever saw her get.

Later I bought a jug of Clorox. It was either that or take a hairbrush to my body. I was getting desperate. I'd gone through a whole bottle of calamine—it did nothing for the itch. The poison oak seemed to be spreading, too, each time I took a shower; I had it everywhere now. Not bothering to dilute the bleach, I poured it on straight. My roommate screamed when she saw me. "What are you doing! It'll scar you!"

"Don't be ridiculous." I didn't know for sure that she was wrong, but if there were scars, they would fade. I stepped on a nail once and I can't even find the place anymore. I have that kind of skin.

Out in front of the dorms, when she told the other girls she had a doctor's appointment that day and would take her own car to the Youth Authority, she could tell Helena didn't believe her.

"Which doctor? You mean you're going off campus?"

"They referred me, yes."

"They never refer anybody. Afraid somebody will find out what quacks they are at the med center — as if it's a secret. What's the matter, Wanda? Is it serious?"

"Not really," Wanda said with the cold little smile she'd practiced in the mirror last night.

"Why bother going at all? God, what an opportunity, a perfectly legit excuse. You could've slept in."

"I think we should get going, Helena. We're late."

Helena took that as an invitation to climb into Wanda's car. "I'd rather you didn't," Wanda said.

"Ride with you?" Helena climbed back out, giving her a queer look, as if searching for evidence of disease. She actually sniffed at Wanda.

"Helena," she said, twisting away. "Don't."

Wanda followed the other girls' car across town and onto 99 South. It had rained last night and was still drizzling, the purplish sky weighing down on the fields like a watercolor done on wet blotter paper. Beneath her skirt she wore no underwear, as John had instructed, and in her pocket was the canister of mace that she'd been carrying in and out of the Youth Authority for the past three weeks — nobody had noticed, the old woman at the front desk merely taking their names so she could phone them in to the professor: roll. Wanda brought the mace not only because John told her to but because she wanted to see if she could, if she'd get caught. Of course not. The old woman always nodded at her sweetly, the guard smiling too, as if about to pat Wanda's curly hair. It was Helena they usually scrutinized, although all of the girls had to empty out their purses for inspection. They wouldn't dare frisk them, much as the professor would probably like that, the girls joked to each other in the car, as a part of their education about the prison system. No doubt he frisked the women he dated, they joked, as a prelude to sex.

HELENA

I was showing Fargo and the other guys the scars on my arm when I glanced over at the lovebirds in their corner. Something about the expressions on their faces. Wanda was sitting on his lap. I quickly looked away. It couldn't be. I almost laughed it was so crazy. We went back to talking about my scars, the usual dumb jokes about let's see the rest of 'em, and I realized we all knew what was going on over there in the corner, the other girls too, but nobody said anything, not even the guys, which made me respect them in an odd way. My face was burnt pink though. I couldn't get over it — Wanda screwing John Mace in front of everybody like this — and it occurred to me I didn't know her at all. I sneaked a look at her face once more to be sure. No doubt about it. Her eyelids were drooping, her mouth slightly open, while Mace stared straight ahead like a dead soldier, the two of them bobbing in their chair ever so slightly.

"How about a game of checkers?" somebody said, and everybody got very busy searching for the board and trying to remember who beat who yesterday and who's up next to play. The other girls and I read each other's faces, silently communicating — are you going to tell or will I? Is this it, then, our last day at the Youth Authority? I was about to stand up, what was the sense in staying, let's get out of here already, let's quit, when Mace rose from the chair, Wanda almost tumbling off his lap. He offered her his hand so she could steady herself — a sort of gentlemanly touch — then zipped himself up. She smoothed her skirt. They left. Just opened the door and left. From the windows we watched as they strolled down the corridor arm in arm. The guard approached them, said a few words; they appeared to be chatting. Mace sprayed him in the face with something, the guard bent over. Mace kicked him in the groin, then he and Wanda were running.

In her car was the shaving cream and razor he'd requested. She'd picked out the most expensive brands — a round, soaplike bar that came with its own mug and brush, and a razor encased in leather — items she'd purchased from a quality men's store rather than a pharmacy or drugstore.

"What's this?" he said when she presented them to him, wrapped in shiny brown paper with yellow ribbon.

"For you, John." She felt herself blushing. "Open it. Maybe you should pull over first." Now she giggled, a gurgling sound to her own ears. Everything sounded that way as they drove farther and farther across the valley — a churning, underwater sound — the vw's frantic, noisy defroster barely keeping up with all the rain, John's nasal humming out of tune with the radio, the balls of her feet pressed against the rubber mat on the passenger's side, the fear in her rolling down her legs and out her toes like waves. And something else, not just fear. A bubbling feeling. Excitement. Love. She'd been shocked when John sprayed the guard's face, though he'd warned her moments before that he would. She hadn't been expecting the kick to the groin, however. Yet she was glad, strangely relieved to see such violence. Including the old woman in the gatehouse getting sprayed, and the other guard too, and her own leg swinging out from her body to kick him in the butt. John had cursed at her for that — was she supposed to just stand there? — then they were running again and she realized John had somehow gotten a gun, probably the gatehouse guard's, the only guard who had a gun at the Youth Authority, and then halfway across the parking lot she remembered John's smashing the stapler against the guard's skull, that was before she'd kicked him. John already had her car keys in his hand, he'd asked her to get them from her purse while they made love, and she'd expected him to use them on her somehow, dig them into her skin to heighten things maybe. But no, he'd wanted the keys for her car, which they ran to, John knowing just what car it was from all her descriptions, yes, she'd described her car just as she had the house she'd grown up in, her neighborhood, what was in her lunch box, John being insatiable for the details of her life. She'd known and not known all these weeks he'd been meaning to escape, somehow using her, how would she ever explain this to anyone?

"Aren't you going to pull over, John?"

"What for?"

She shook the present at him. "Right," he said. He was doing sixty now and they were on back roads, muddy but straight roads that met at right angles as if for some purpose, when really they were out in the middle of nowhere. He turned down another road and they skidded to a stop, mud splattering the windshield. "Now what," he said.

"Your present," Wanda said.

He tore it open, ribbon dangling from his knee. "Why didn't you just get me shaving cream like I asked?"

"I got you something special," she said quietly.

"You need water for this."

"I know that, John."

He held out the cup. "Get me some water. Please."

How like him to add the please at the end. "John. Can't you just wait till later?"

He stripped off his shirt. "Get me some water, will you?"

"Where?"

He handed her the mug. "See that slough over there?"

"What about rainwater?"

"I want it from the slough."

The water from the slough was dark as coffee, dank, fetid. She slipped in mud and grass and wondered, of course, what was she doing here. Let him take the car, her money, anything; instead, this seemed an inescapable culmination, a love act she had to go on with no matter how it sickened her. "Here's your water," she said on returning and watched him mix it with the soap into a light brown lather.

"Did you bring the scissors?" he said.

"In the glove compartment." She was getting irritated yet more numb by the minute, her life over, college over with, no more friends, family, as if she'd been waiting for this awful time every day since childhood. "What are you doing, John?"

He set the mug on the dashboard and began cutting his hair, crude, ragged hunks of it falling to the floor. "Get those, will you? Throw them out the window."

"What are you doing?"

"You'll see." He laughed and she almost laughed too. If Helena could see her now. She hated herself, how she hated herself; she reached for the scissors when he was through.

"Get away from those," he said.

"Why?"

"Because." Now he was lathering up his scalp, then shaving, glancing in the rear-view mirror as though he did this every morning of his life. He cut himself, the blood trickling onto his ear, but Wanda couldn't feel anymore and didn't comment. "Now," he said. "Something to dry off with." She saw him inspecting her blouse.

"No," she said.

He dabbed at his head with his white T-shirt, then tossed it at her. "Give me your shirt. You wear this."

"You want to wear a blouse with flowers on it? Why are you doing this?"

"Just give me the shirt."

His T-shirt felt soft as it met her skin. He hadn't even noticed the lace brassiere she'd worn, though it no longer mattered.

He started up the car.

"Where to now?" she said.

"It's a surprise."

"I bet." She felt in her element, dirty, wet, cold. "You know I'd really like something to drink," she said. "Could we stop at a liquor store?"

"No."

"Where are you taking me? Where are we going?"

"You'll find out, little girl." He gazed at her, his green eyes huge and flaming against his bald head, her flowered blouse buttoned wrong across his chest.

"This is crazy," she said. "Shaving your head, my blouse. If it's to disguise yourself, well, you look so noticeable. Nobody will forget your face, John."

They were coming to a town, no, some houses. Strange, a neighborhood and nothing else, no gas station, no stores. Just a strip of houses on a couple of streets, crummy houses, shacks, trailer homes plopped down at skewed angles, and nobody around, no children, no dogs. The rain had stopped, the sun came out, and Wanda felt hopeful again. They were going to his parents, or to some friends. John stopped at a corner — well, it would be a corner anywhere else. Here it was just some weeds and part of an old picket fence.

"What?" Wanda said over the vw's idle, her whole body vibrating in time with the engine. The sun disappeared into a blanket of fog that seemed almost to seep upward from the ground.

"Get out."

"Out?"

"Out."

She opened the door and stood uncertainly. "Take your purse," he said. "And this, and this." He threw things out the door, the mug, the soap, books of hers from the back seat, a sweater. He kept the scissors and razor. The gun, which she'd forgotten about till now, was still in the glove compartment where he'd put it hours ago, wrapped in her scarf.

"Now close your eyes," he said.

She did.

"And breathe. Breathe in through your nose and out your mouth. Again. Keep breathing, faster now. Imagine something — something nice."

Nothing came to mind at first, the air around her damp and close, the fog itself a place that was soft and nice, all past deceits and sorrows gone and lost, as lost as she was now. The car door slammed. She could hear it faintly, feel the force of it swirling particles of fog and air toward her as he drove off. She opened her eyes after a moment and from one of the houses a woman emerged, a woman in an apron with wide thick arms, her hair in a bubble atop her head. She headed down the steps toward Wanda, who sat down dreamily, watching the shape approach, this shape that seemed to float.

They tracked her down finally, after quizzing me and the other girls and searching her room for clues. She'd taken the bus south to her parents, just told them she'd dropped out, I guess. I don't know what she told them about her car. Right away she got the job at Lucky's; that's where the police found her. She wrote me a letter about it, how after a few days of sitting in the sheriff's office and answering questions, they let her go, didn't arrest her, no probation or anything. She'd gotten on very well with the officers, in fact, making them coffee and answering their phones.

I called her. "Wanda," I said, "you've got to change. Stop being so nice. This experience almost ruined your life."

"Helena." She paused, maybe thinking something over. "Don't say it just happened to me. It happened to you too. Something happened to you because of this."

I felt like a building with its side blown out, both ugly and delirious with possibility, open to the sky. The day before, I'd slept with the professor. We were talking about Wanda in his office — I told him the whole story — when he said, leaning forward in his chair, which creaked knowingly, "You're confused, aren't you?" Later, in bed, he traced the faint scars across my arms and back, murmuring as though he understood me now, believing I'd received those scars in childhood. That I was one of the disadvantaged.

I didn't tell him otherwise.

The police never did find Mace, although Wanda's car showed up in some mountain town, parked in front of the five and dime. You'd think somebody would remember seeing a guy with a bald head in a flowered blouse, but no. Maybe he bought a wig. In any case they stopped looking for him, Wanda says. He's not dangerous. He doesn't even know how to use a gun, and anyway, he left it behind in the glove compartment. She knows all this because she's dating a police officer now and he tells her everything.

MY MARILYN

She lives in Salmon, Idaho, and works as a bartender.

But now she's sitting across from me at the Valley Hunt Club, Pasadena, California — a garden wedding reception.

Marilyn Marlowe. In grade school she wore boys sneakers with dresses. And because she did, we did. Boat shoes, we called them. She played two-square better than anyone, even the boys, all of whom were in love with her. So were the girls. Seal brown eyes, white blond hair in a pixie cut, and her skin . . . so shadowy pale, exactly like shadows on the snow, we agreed, though most of us had never seen snow. Marilyn Monroe, Marilyn Marlowe: was it any coincidence their names sounded alike? Or so we whispered to each other in the girls' bathroom, hands over our mouths, nails filed short so as not to wreck our two-square game. *Because Marilyn did.*

This table at the Valley Hunt Club has a white linen cloth, a centerpiece of roses and baby's breath, lit candles — and is swarming with people here to see Marilyn. Curiosity seekers. She hasn't been back in nine years. Rumor has it she showed up unexpectedly the week before the wedding, to visit. She and the bride used to be close friends. Used to be. From the way the bride keeps glancing over here, you can tell she wishes she hadn't invited Marilyn. This is a formal wedding yet Marilyn is wearing a jean skirt, white tights, and clogs. But what she has on isn't the real problem; it's how she's acting.

"Ted! Peter!" she screams at the top of her lungs. "Sammy! Gimme a kiss!"

Long wet kisses you can hear from this side of the table, while the women and some of the men stare down at their silverware. "Where's the champagne?" she crows. "I want another drinkie."

In no time she's hanging all over Bob Burnell, whose skinny, cold-faced wife is pretending to talk to Jim Argus, pretending not to notice Marilyn's arms around her husband's neck. As for the other women, each is holding onto some part of her husband's anatomy and chattering gaily, nervously.

I have nothing to worry about. Marilyn can't steal my husband because I don't have one. Tonight, I don't even have a date. I get up and wander over by the buffet, the pool, then back toward the tables, a couple of feet away from Marilyn and Bob Burnell. I can see her hand under the table. "Come on, Bobby." Giggling. She moves her hand up his leg and he laughs clumsily, clearing his throat.

They say she's been doing this all week, going after men, married, single, it doesn't matter. What I can't figure out is why the men are falling for it. Marilyn Marlowe is no longer pretty. Her face is thick and her skin sags loose, like heavy draperies. Her teeth are bad; she never had braces like the rest of us.

Yet I do understand so perfectly. Marilyn Marlowe's hair is still white blond and very, very fine — like the hair of the Swedish dolls my grandmother used to give me. "Swedish," she'd say, "like you, Kirsten, dear." I'd hug the dolls by the head, so in love was I with their hair. "Don't touch," my grandmother would say. "They're not that kind of doll." And into the glass cabinet they would go, leaving me to stand forlornly, watching them, locked out. "Here," she would say, taking pity and handing me a rag doll, which I'd drop, kick, hug, talk to, yell at, draw on, sleep with.

We all want to hug Marilyn Marlowe by the head.

Look at the way we've arranged ourselves around this table, all the chairs facing hers. People talk to each other but with one ear cocked, waiting. Whenever she speaks it is strangely silent: everybody stops what they're saying to hear what *she* will say.

In grade school she hardly ever talked; she didn't need to. But when she did, oh, that nasal voice, that slur, as if she couldn't be bothered opening her mouth all the way.

Now it sounds like a speech impediment.

"So I said, lemme fix you a drink, and she said, you get your hands off my husband, you pussy — "

Everyone at the table winces. The language, so crude. This is Marilyn Marlowe? Bob Burnell smiles at her, slightly bug-eyed; his wife is nowhere to be seen.

"Great reception," the man next to me says. Somebody I went to school with, I think, though I can't remember his name.

"Great." I nod and he goes back to his roast beef, picking it up with his fingers and stuffing it into a roll. His elbows strain against the sleeves of his suit jacket, yet his fingers are delicate, like a raccoon's. He sees me staring at him.

"Were you a cheerleader?" he says.

"No," I answer, and we turn away from each other.

■ Salmon, Idaho. I've never been there, but I can picture the rutted road through the center of it, aluminum-siding houses strewn about on either side. Bare lots. The wind is blowing, there's trash spinning down the street, caught in chicken-wire fences. The bar has a neon sign: Rosie's. The *o* and the *e* don't light. I hear that Marilyn's sister lives in Salmon too, with her three kids and construction-worker husband. So does another girl we went to school with, Joanne Sprock, divorced and remarried now; they say her new husband beats her.

In Salmon, Idaho, it's always cold, even in summer, and the sun, how it shines—a mean, hard sun all year round. But the beauty, there must be beauty: a wall of pines in the distance, the mountains sheer and aloof. The snow is powdery, leaves a sweet dry taste in your mouth . . .

"Bobby, you were always so strong," Marilyn says. It sounds like "stwong," and is she teasing him? Bob Burnell was always pencil-thin, socially awkward. He's thrilled about the compliment, though, bobbing in his seat like a corn thresher—no one, no one ever called him Bobby before. Not his mother. Not his sharp-hipped wife. Fool that he is, I'm happy he's happy; Marilyn has made him happy.

Fools that we all are. If he weren't talking to her, I would be. Not that she'd recognize me, I look so different now, taller and more angular than the plump sweet thing I was in high school, always in skirts and knee socks and loafers. A good girl. The kind who stayed up all night painting signs for the Pep Club while everyone else slept.

"I can't dance with you, Bobby." Bobby. Like an endearment. "But you go ahead," Marilyn says. "Dance with your wife, Bobby."

And he does. First he has to track her down, off in a corner with Jim Argus; Bob glares at Jim, taps his wife on the shoulder, and they dance. Their bodies are glued together at the hips. Marilyn watches them, smiling faintly, then goes up to another man, Dirk Spencer. "I always loved you, Dirky." It sounds like "dirty." They go sit at her spot at the table, their heads bent together. I want to hear what they're saying but the music grows suddenly louder. People dance wildly. The table is virtually empty now, just the two of them and the man next to me eating roast beef. "Another beer, please," he says, raising an arm for the waiter. Then to me, when the waiter ignores him, "Guess you're supposed to get your own." He shrugs and continues eating.

"What made you think I was a cheerleader?" I ask.

"I didn't mean it as an insult. I just thought maybe you were. What do I know? I used to hang out in the parking lot and smash car windows for fun, with a baseball bat. Did I ever do that to your car?"

"Not that I recall."

"Good," he says. "But if I ever did, I'm sorry."

Dirk stands up with two empty glasses. Off to get refills. First he leans over and says something in Marilyn's ear. He kisses her neck.

I stand up.

"Anyway," the man says, wiping his fingers on the napkin one by one, as if polishing silver, "I'm a nice person now. Very respectable. You want to dance?"

"Later, maybe."

Dirk leaves and I take his place, next to Marilyn. "I was thinking about that tree in the playground," I say. "At elementary school, remember? I think it was a pepper tree." She stares at me. *Who are you, bitch.* "And that hill by the pepper tree, how we all used to run down it. The boys chased the girls who pretended to be horses. The boys pretended to be planes, remember? I guess you don't remember me. Kirsten Nelson."

"You always wore your hair in braids," she says.

"All during high school, too." Now my hair is what they call sculptured; I put this foam on it and arrange it with my fingers.

Marilyn won't even look at me. I follow her gaze: Dirk is talking to a woman with a clutch bag coyly pressed to her body. The empty glasses, the refills, are nowhere around. "Asshole," Marilyn says.

I move my chair closer. "What's it like in Salmon, Idaho? What made you decide to move there?"

"I needed a job." I wait for her to go on. She doesn't.

"Is it in the mountains?"

"The mountains!" She laughs. "I can't even dance anymore."

"You can't dance?"

"I had this operation. Varicose veins, can you believe it? At my age? That's why I have to wear these." She pulls at her white stockings.

"I'm sorry to hear that," I say.

"You're *sorry?*" She smooths out the tablecloth. "I didn't mean to say that. It's not your fault."

I watch a waiter trying to kill a bee with a fly swatter. From somewhere else, a burst of laughter. "I had another operation, too," she says softly.

The band plays a peculiar-sounding waltz, off balance like a record going at the wrong speed. "Yeah," she says, "another operation. They shaved my pussy bald for that one."

I swallow. My mouth is dry, all the water glasses are empty.

"I know what you're thinking," she says.

"You do?"

"My pussy hair is blond."

"That's not what I—"

"All the men want to know that," she says. "Even when they don't ask, you can tell that's what they want to know. What they really want to know. That's the first thing they go for, too. Not my tits, not my ass."

She was the first one to go steady. Fifth grade, Mark Steele. I remember the day it happened, I even remember what she was wearing—a brown and red plaid matching skirt and blouse, white piping on the collar and sleeves. And the boat shoes. Mark Steele's I.D. bracelet on her wrist.

"Men are so dirty," Marilyn says, "don't you think? Sometimes I look at their eyes and I think even their eyes are sweating, you know what I mean?"

"No, I—"

"You can't even carry on a conversation, you're so nervous. Jesus." She gets up from the table and storms off. "I'll get my own goddamn drink!" she says to no one in particular.

I remember something else. Did I hear it, dream it? Make it up? That Marilyn Marlowe's parents beat her. With sticks from their garden. They hurled them at her, struck them across the backs of her thighs, beat her little girl's stomach like a drum. Just as I used to fear my own parents beating me. They wanted to; I could see it in my mother's eyes when she spanked me with the hairbrush, the back of it—how she wanted to turn it over, turn me over, crack open my chest with the bristles of a brush. And my father. *Goddamn it to hell.* Banging pipes under the sink with a wrench; his rage came out when he fixed things, which he broke instead. Windows, light fixtures, plumbing. *Sonofabitch, goddamn it to hell.*

"I'm back," Marilyn says gaily, as if we've been friends forever. Then, more darkly, "You're stuck with me now. No one else wants me."

"That's not true."

That's not true," she mimics. She slurps at her drink, picks out an ice cube, throws it into the bushes. "What about him?" She points to the man with the roast beef.

"What about him?"

"He's cute. Hey, do I know you?" she says to him. "You're cute. Can I sit in your lap?"

He gets up and leaves the table. Disappears through a gate.

"Shit," Marilyn says. "Shit! Idiot."

"Who's an idiot?" Me? The man who just left?

"Me." She pinches the flesh on her arm. "Me. I'm a fucking idiot. Jesus, my life!"

My parents laughing drunkenly, looming over me.

"Can't you move?" I say to Marilyn. "Can't you—" She stares at me, begins to laugh. "I don't know," I continue, "you could go back to school. Start over."

I almost laugh too. Start over?

She leans over and pats me on the cheek. "Thanks," she says.

"Don't thank me."

"Ohhh," she moans, tilting back in her chair, head rolling.

"Are you all right?"

"I wanna get fucked. That's all I want." She looks at me, one eye shut, and enunciates: "I ... just ... wanna ... get ... fucked."

A man walks by. "Do you want to fuck me?" she calls out to him. He laughs, shakes his head, keeps walking. "Come back here!" she yells. "Hey! I wanna fuck!"

"Marilyn," I say.

She turns on me. "Listen, bitch face, shut up. Just shut up. I know all about you."

"What do you know?" I imagine myself hollowed out on the inside, as you would scoop seeds from a cantaloupe. "There's nothing to know," I say.

"Yeah," she says, "nothing to know. No secrets. You know the worst part? My hair's falling out." She laughs. "The hair on my *head*. Big clumps."

I'm silent. I thought we were talking about me. We were.

"Next they want to take my boobs." She looks at mine and smiles. "Cut them off," she says.

"Marilyn," I say finally. "What exactly is — "

"What's wrong with me. That's what you want to know."

I move my tongue around my mouth, as if I'll find some moisture there. She's so close she could kiss me. "Who do you think you are?" she says under her breath. "Who the hell are you?"

I stand up but she pulls me back down by the wrist. "What's it like being so goddamn happy?" She touches one of the stiff little curls on my head. "That's what I used to wonder. You and your braids. How much did they have to pay you to look so happy?"

"Who?"

"Your parents."

"I wasn't happy."

"Not happy." She pushes me away and reaches for her drink. "Let's talk about something else," she says. "Let's talk about you and your husband."

"I'm not married."

"Let's talk about your sex life."

"No."

"Come on," she says. "I love talking about sex, don't you? Tell me." She leans towards me, bourbon breath. "Does he fuck you every night?"

"I don't have a husband. I told you."

"So I'm right. You're turning red. He fucks you every night. Who would've thought when we were little girls that *your* husband would fuck you every night."

"I'm not even seeing anybody."

She grabs my arm. "He fucks you every night. He fucks your cunt and you love it. *I* love it. I wanna get fucked."

"Let go." I'm trying to remove her hand from my arm but Marilyn digs in with her nails; I think of her hands, her fingers falling off and tumbling into darkness.

She jiggles my arm. "Where'd he go?"

"Who?"

"What's-his-name. Dick, Dirk. Where's my drink? *Where's my drink!*" She stands up screaming, still holding my arm as if it's hers now. "Who are these people?"

"Marilyn, sit down."

"Who *are* these people?"

With my free hand, I tug on her skirt, then her arm, until I gently persuade her down into her seat. "Let's go inside, all right, Marilyn? Marilyn?" I reach for her hair, meaning to pat her head, I think, to hold her, soothe her. But when I touch the white blondness, the slightest touch, a clump of it falls out into my palm. "Oh, Marilyn, your hair."

"My hair?"

"It fell out."

"Yes," she says. "It fell out."

I'm still holding the hair next to her scalp, as if I can put it back. Then, guiltily, I slip the hair into my pocket, not knowing what else to do with it. "Shall we go inside?"

I pull her to her feet and she leans against me staggering as we go in through the French doors, past a dining room filled with guests, into a central hallway with its winding staircase, then finally a dark green sitting room with wall sconces and potted palms. I close the door, while Marilyn finds the couch, lies down.

I sit beside her, feeling the hair in my pocket, weirdly soft and thin. I say her name, whisper it.

"Was that my name you said?" Her voice is thick, lazy, childlike.

"Yes. Marilyn."

She draws my head down towards her own. "I love it when they say your name. You know what I mean." She murmurs in my ear, something else, I'm not sure what. *Free me?*

I kiss her, sliding my tongue into her mouth.

"No, not that. This." She reaches between my legs. "Oh," she says, her hand flapping around, searching. "Oh shit." She begins to laugh, crazily. "Seems I've made a little mistake," she says.

I imagine an erection like a stalk pressed between us, secret and protected. For her sake.

But she is falling asleep in my arms.

THE SAN JUANS ARE BEAUTIFUL

Her cousin had eloped, so at the last minute Nance had to fill in as an elderly lady's companion on a boating trip to the San Juans—a lady she knew only slightly, a friend of the family, who showed up on holidays, Christmas or the Fourth of July, to survey the doings. A chair would be drawn up for her, and in stony silence she would watch the children in concert. Or children would be presented to her: "Ellie, you remember little Matthew," little Matthew gently shoved forth by one or the other of his parents for inspection, which Ellie would undertake as though judging a flower show, cocking her head this way and that: "How old did you say?"

"Matthew is five now."

"In school yet?"

"Next year, Ellie."

And Matthew would squirm until his father or mother anchored his foot with one of their own to keep him there, whispering commands in his ear: "Ask Ellie if she's enjoying her Christmas. Say thank you."

Ellie had her own children, grown of course, practically senior citizens themselves, a son and a daughter who lived far enough away for them not to bring her out regularly for holidays. Fine by her, Ellie said. It upset her, she claimed, witnessing their daily lives—her children and their children and now *their* children. Couldn't stand to see them do things that way. Live in that house. Keep those dogs. Throw away money like that. Their jobs, their neighborhoods, the schools they sent their children to! Here she would moan, as though those around her understood, when in fact the Johnson clan knew little of Ellie's children, barely their names; Nance's own newlywed parents had moved into the neighborhood long after Ellie's children had been shipped off to boarding schools and college and finally off to marriage and their own families, practically never to be seen in the neighborhood again.

■ The cabins on the little cruise ship (it slept only forty, including employees) were of two kinds: those on the very top deck—the staterooms—and those off the dining room like Ellie's, tiny cabins such as you would expect on a boat, barely enough room to turn around. Toilet, sink, stand-up shower. A small porthole that could be propped open, the bed next to it. This was where Ellie spent her days, reading novels, occasionally squinting at the view. "Strawberry Island," she'd say, waving her book. "Lovely island. They used to stop there until the dock fell in."

"What are you reading?" Nance inquired. There was no place for her to sit, so she would stand, towering over Ellie though she herself was short, bumping her head if the boat swayed. It was either that or sit next to Ellie, something she'd never do. She hardly knew her, though she'd known her all her life. "What are you reading, Ellie?"

"Oh, trash."

Indeed, she saw that this was true. *Passion in Marseilles.* On the blueblack cover, a woman in a red dress pouted, her decolletage brimming over with bosom, the man at her side seemingly staring down into her cleavage. Nance remembered something she'd heard about Ellie—that she went to dirty movies. Some sort of continual misunderstanding; she'd think the movie was about something else, then would stay because she'd paid her money. Meeting Ellie's daughter several years ago at a family gathering (Nance's family; Ellie's never gathered), Nance had overheard her say to someone, "With Mother, everything is sex."

Ellie pressed her face to the porthole. "Is that a whale?"

"The wrong season, isn't it?" Nance picked up the book and glanced at a page. Somebody's breasts spilling out, a man burying his head in them—for some reason the awful prose excited her.

Ellie turned toward her, the porthole fogged up. "It is a whale," she said triumphantly.

"Really, how exciting, Ellie." Nance knew it was not a whale. The announcer or master of ceremonies or whatever you called him—the blond guy who sat on a bar stool with a mike and told bad jokes and commented on the scenery—had said there were few whales nowadays, they'd been hunted from these waters, just porpoises now, "for the *porpoise* of saying hello to you on your beautiful cruise of the San Juans." The other guests, none of whom was a day under seventy, had laughed appreciatively.

"Go up on deck and see," Ellie told Nance. "Give me back my book. Go have fun, now. I didn't bring you to sit with me, not that there's anywhere to sit. Go have fun." She fanned the book at her. The cleavage of the woman on the cover appeared to glimmer and shake. "Go."

Nance wondered if Ellie had invented the whale just to get rid of her. Entirely possible.

She backed out of the room, recalling a whale-watching expedition she'd gone on once, at the entrance of Scanlon's Bay in Mexico: one barnacle-encrusted gray whale swam beneath another, a female, and balanced her aloft, while a third, a male, attempted to penetrate her, his long floundering penis visible in the foamy turbulence. An unwieldy operation, it was how they mated due to their size, their waterboundness, the fact they were mammals; it took the cooperation of three and many, many tries. A rare thing to witness, the guide had said. A beautiful thing, a clumsy thing.

Nance hesitated at the stairs leading to the main deck. She could go up to the deck and stroll, promenade. Pace. Or she could go up another flight to her room and sit. She was the youngest person here, aside from the twenty-year-olds who worked on board preparing meals, fetching drinks, tidying cabins, washing down the decks, curling rope into piles, pointing out views to the guests, chitchatting. Even the captain seemed young, younger than herself possibly, and she was between her twenties and thirties — this was how she thought of herself — schooled beyond need and employed in the family enterprise, Simpleman's Office Supplies, which was why she'd been able to get away on such short notice.

"For Ellie," her father had said, restocking Xerox paper, "go. She's done so much for you kids." Checks for their birthdays, trips such as this one. Nance remembered a sweater Ellie had given her as a child; it had red satin ribbon woven in and out where the buttons should be. "There's no reason for you to stay," her father had said. "Is there?" A remark on her marital status, or lack thereof: unattached, aside from an old boyfriend she'd lately begun to see — was that why Ellie had invited her? So she could meet a suitor? But who was she supposed to meet?

Three cousins and her sister had accompanied Ellie on cruises at one time or another — on the same cruise, she believed, through the San Juans, though one had gone on to Alaska. They seemed reluctant to talk about it. "The San Juans are beautiful," her sister had said, "but damp, rainy." And? So? That was all. She hadn't had time to grill her sister more, this trip being so hastily arranged. Ellie went on the same cruise each year, staying in the same cabin; the help knew and liked her. Of course they liked her: she crushed five-dollar bills into their hands at every opportunity, a habit Nance found discomfiting, embarrassing — she would stand off to the side pretending to enjoy the view. *The San Juans are beautiful.* Ellie kept throwing money at her, too — tipping her for coming along? What was she to spend it on? Souvenirs and trinkets? Cocktails? She did spend it on cocktails, which weren't covered in the price of the cruise, cocktails she drank in her stateroom alone. Margaritas, Tanqueray and tonic—last night she'd sampled a martini.

Now she ordered another one and headed for her room.

No mere cabin, this: Ellie had engaged for her the very best state-room, on the top deck, with windows all around, table and chairs, a desk, a double bed.

"Shouldn't it be the other way around?" Nance had asked Ellie when shown to the room. Her cousins, her sister, hadn't mentioned this. "Shouldn't you take this room and I'll stay below?"

Ellie winked. "Have fun," she'd said, slipping her a five, and stumped out of the room. She wore galoshes up to her shins, the kind with buckles; she wore two purses with gold chains for straps slung across her chest, like ammo on a grenadier; she bandied a cane. "Have fun."

■ Amid the bald-pated gentlemen, age spots on their heads like maps of the Old World, and their scarved wives, tiny and dressed in white jackets with gold buttons, and Keds that looked too large, there was one couple close to her age—or only ten years older: a man and his very pregnant wife. Their last fling, they said, before parenthood.

They drank in everything: the view, the folklore, the jokes barked out by the blond master of ceremonies. They laughed harder than any-one, the wife until tears ran down her face.

"The hormones," she said to Nance, who sat next to her at the bar. "They're playing me like a slide whistle."

"I know," Nance said.

"You have children?"

"My cousins, my sister . . ." Each of them, she realized, within a year after this cruise, had found a mate, married, and conceived. As for herself—well, sometimes it almost seemed as though she might have children, might have had them and forgotten somehow. Those dreams she'd had recently, a baby in her arms, the baby gone suddenly, she'd left it on a bench or in a store.

"How old are you?" the woman asked.

Only pregnant women and the elderly, it seemed, thought they could ask you anything. "Twenty-nine."

"Yeah, right. Me too." She sipped seltzer and munched one carrot stick after another from a nearby vegetable tray.

"No, I really am twenty-nine."

"I thought you meant the joke." At Nance's blank look she said, "I've been twenty-nine each year since turning thirty."

"That joke." Then she realized she *had* lied, unintentionally, about her own age. A slip of the tongue. She was thirty, closer to thirty-one. How could she forget? It was something she thought about nearly every minute.

"So how old are you?" she asked the woman.

"Eleven years older than you and about to be an unwed mother."

"That isn't your husband with you?"

"We're live-ins."

Nance smiled politely, the term sounding more like a job, as in live-in help. In her family, people didn't live together, nor did they divorce. They married young. They married for life.

"There's my common law!" the woman crowed, waving him over. "Have you met? Bob, this is—"

"Nance."

He was wearing a white turtleneck sweater, tucked in, the same as he always wore. Probably he'd made the same mistake as Nance: the weather overcast and misty—this was the Northwest after all—she'd brought the wrong clothes and had been wearing the same gray, hooded sweatshirt every day over her sundresses and tank tops and shorts. Wishing she'd at least brought another pair of socks. She didn't dare wash them, they'd never dry in the dampness. Her sister had warned her to bring warm clothes, but Nance had chosen not to listen. Cruises meant sunshine and warmth. Nobody went on cruises to cold places.

"We never did introduce ourselves," the pregnant woman said. "I'm—"

She was cut off by the master of ceremonies, back from his break now: "That fantastic island on your left, my friends, is known as the island of the woman. Note the two hills parallel to each other, rising at points — legend has it a woman laid down to entertain her lover here and fainted from the pleasure. Bella Island, folks. Isn't it bea-*oo*-tee-ful?"

"Does he make this stuff up himself?" Nance said, but both the pregnant woman and Bob put fingers to their lips; they wanted to hear.

"If we could fly overhead — " the MC continued, dipping a shoulder, hand skimming the air, "— if we could fly, folks, we'd see the whole island is shaped like a woman. Shoulders. Chest. Waist. Hips." He curved his hand through the air to demonstrate a shape like a Barbie doll's; he actually raised one eyebrow. "Ooo-la-la."

"Jesus Christ," Nance said.

"I think he's kind of cute," the pregnant woman said.

"Me too," said Bob.

Ellie emerged from the stairwell, cane swinging, purses crisscrossing her chest. "Excuse me," Nance said and rose, thinking she should go to her. But Ellie didn't like to be bothered. Nothing angered her as much as people making a fuss. Still: Ellie seldom came out except at sunset, to walk the deck and hand out five-dollar tips. It wasn't sunset now, but nearly lunchtime. So why was she on deck? Meals Ellie liked to eat in her room, on her bed, reading her books; Nance had tried to dine with her there — it was awkward, she'd had to eat standing up, her tray on the dresser — until Ellie threw her out. "There's no room for you here! Eat out there where you belong!"

Ellie clumped along in her galoshes, purse chains jangling. Everyone cleared out of the way.

"Who is that?" Bob said. He was mostly bald, only a thin swatch of hair left, growing in the vaguely obscene shape of a triangle. "I don't think we've seen her before, have we?"

"She's kind of like an aunt," Nance said, rising to go to her after all. "Friend of the family, hard to explain. It's who I came with."

■ "Are you all right?" she asked Ellie. "Can I get you something?"

"Fine, fine. My hands are tingling, so I decided to come up. Is that Bella Island?"

"Your hands are tingling?" Stroke. Heart Attack. Ellie dying in her room, or right here at Nance's feet. Buried at sea wrapped in a sail: all Nance's fault. "Maybe you ought to sit down. Can I get you some water?"

"Is that Bella Island?"

"The one shaped like a woman," Nance said, casting about for help. Did a cruise ship this size even have a doctor? "I think you should sit down, Ellie." Trying to sound firm or at least calm. She kept thinking: Ellie is eighty-five years old, she could go in a second. She did seem pale.

"He makes that up, you know," Ellie said. "It's not called Bella Island. It's Clark Island and it's shaped nothing like a woman."

Suddenly a chair appeared. "For you, madame." The master of ceremonies, naturally; who else would say something so corny? Relieved, annoyed, Nance said, "Thank you."

He managed to charm Ellie into sitting down, something Nance would never have been able to do. He kneeled at Ellie's side, got her to describe the tingling.

"It's a tingling," Ellie said. "A tingling, don't you understand? Both my hands, just my hands."

Nance hadn't seen the MC up close before. Blond and baby-faced, he was almost pretty—the sort elderly women found irresistible.

He asked Ellie if she needed to see a doctor.

"For a tingling in my hands? My land, no!"

The MC looked directly at Nance. "Well," he said, "what can we do?" He did have nice eyes. Blue, of course. Long lashes. He really was pretty, like a china figurine. She found herself wanting to flirt with him, though he repelled her. She liked dark men, tall men, brooding men.

"It won't do to insist," Nance said. Then to Ellie: "Are they tingling now?"

She shook her hands, peered at them. "They're not. A fine day it's turning into. Look, the sun!" She jabbed the air with her entire hand, the fingers straight and stiff and pointed together.

The fog cleaved away from the sun, so fast it appeared the sun was falling. People shielded their eyes.

Ellie was persuaded to join the others for lunch, but not before she managed to slip a five-dollar bill into the shirt pocket of the MC, whose name, Nance learned, was Chad.

■ Ellie and Nance ate with Bob and his pregnant live-in, and the MC as well, who continually got up to make announcements on his portable mike: about the islands they passed, about gratuities already being included, about bingo that night and a dance the next.

Each time he returned and sat down, he squeezed in a little closer to Nance. Her face flushed pink. The heat of his body, the warmth of this room, the food. Steak, hot soup, rolls, coffee. The conviviality, the schnapps: the MC now appeared handsome to her, desirable even, and by the same token Ellie's years seemed to lessen, her wrinkles softened, her skin tone lit from within and ivory, like the brooch on her blue silk dress.

"I'm so full I feel stupid," Ellie said, blinking her eyes. "Like a snake with a big lump, couldn't move for weeks."

"How are your hands now?" Nance asked. "Do you think we ought check in with a doctor at the next port?"

"No, no, and *no*." She was fiddling with one of her purses, getting out a five.

"Please, Ellie, please — no more money. You don't have to pay me for being here. You've done enough, more than enough. I'm delighted, I'm grateful — "

"This isn't for you," Ellie said, looking around for their server. "It's for that girl. I don't see her, do you?"

"No."

"I'm going to my room. You give it to her." Ellie smoothed the bill onto the table, a domestic gesture, as though freshening a pillow or straightening bedcovers.

"I will." Nance waited until Ellie was gone, then excused herself to the live-in couple — the MC was busy with yet another announcement — and stood to leave, anticipating the walk she would take on deck, the sky, the ocean, an icy blue against the white of the boat. She left the five where it was.

"When will I see you again?" sang the MC into the mike. A song of his own making, apparently; she'd never heard the tune before, although the lyrics were familiar. Too familiar. "Oh Nance, when will I see you again?"

Elderly heads turned to gaze at her with curiosity and longing.

"Bob," the pregnant woman said, "you never sing to me anymore." He whistled a bit, then laid his balding head to rest on her bosom. She kissed the hair that was remaining.

■ The next day was gorgeous too. The same brilliant sky and sun that caused one to feel dizzy, off-center; shadows fell at wrong angles — nature had made a willful mistake.

Today they would stop at Orcas Island, named for the small whales seen in these waters almost three centuries ago, so Chad announced as the ship bumped against the dock and ground its engines back and forth. Finally Nance had a purpose: to escort Ellie around the town and harbor. Ellie said she wanted to find her sister a necklace. Usually during dock visits she stayed on board, reading in her cabin and waving Nance off with admonitions to "have fun."

They were the last persons off. Ellie refused anyone's help in getting down the wood steps placed next to the ship — not only Nance's help, but that of the very pleasant twenty-year-old who routinely assisted all the passengers off. Nor would she accept the help of the captain or the MC: "I want to do this myself."

In addition to all her purses, her cane, and her galoshes, she wore a poncho. "Better coverage than a mackintosh," she'd told Nance as they'd waited to disembark.

"But, Ellie, it's so sunny."

"I don't want to hear it! I come here every year, and every year on one of these dock visits somebody gets drenched. Drenched! I'm even equipped with an umbrella," she confided.

"You are?"

"Inside." She tapped one of her purses; a gold chain jingled prettily. "It folds up small."

Nance recalled what Ellie had told her before this trip, explaining why her purses had chains, not straps: "Straps they'll cut; chains they can't." Meaning thieves.

Now Ellie sat on the edge of the boat arranging her purses, legs splayed on the wooden steps.

"Can't I at least hold something for you?" Nance said. "Your cane?"

Tucking the cane in amongst her purses, Ellie turned and painstakingly crawled down the steps backwards, poncho and skirts riding up over her knees.

"She does this every year," the MC whispered. "Horrifying, isn't it?"

Ellie's exit from the boat was the beginning of the longest two hours Nance had ever spent. Ellie walked slow and talked loud and had to stop frequently to check through her purses — for a map, for her umbrella (had she brought it or did she just think she had?), for money to give to the children she saw (Nance cringed), for her sister's earrings, which the necklace she would buy must match.

After an hour they had yet to stop at a single store; they'd hardly made it down the street. Nance suggested that since they weren't getting much shopping done, they might stop at a clinic and let the doctor examine Ellie's hands, only to have Ellie inform her that the tingling had been a result of reading in one position too long — and would she please mind her own business.

"Certainly." Nance tried to appreciate the view: it was stunning. Up on hills against a blue sky stood white frame houses, their porches hung with baskets of fuchsia. Everywhere she looked were pine trees and wild blackberries. The berries grew like weeds here; even on the main street you couldn't help but step on the occasional blackberry when avoiding a puddle.

Ellie was ecstatic about the puddles. "See? This is why I wear galoshes!"

"Yes, it's a very good idea," Nance murmured, her neck tight, nerves strained. "Would you like to go into this store here? They might carry necklaces."

Inside, Ellie opened a coin purse, took out the ball of tissue paper that held her sister's earrings, and unwrapped them. They were small white porcelain globes with a painted-on design of tiny pink flowers, very delicate; brass backings. "Do you have a necklace to match?" she asked the clerk, hair in a bun, fiftyish and plump, who unlocked a glass cabinet and removed from it a tray of necklaces, gold, silver, polished stone, even one made of glittery gems.

There wasn't one that matched. Nance ventured a question about Ellie's sister — was she older or younger? — only to learn she was dead.

"I promised her the necklace," Ellie said, "so I continue to look."

"Really." Nance didn't know what else to say.

As they returned to the ship, clouds were building. "What did I tell you?" Ellie said. "Any minute it's going to storm."

"Is that so." Nance felt dull, claustrophobic: the thought of getting on the boat again. This boat, any boat. She'd gladly stand out in a pouring rain. After seeing Ellie to her room, she hurried off the boat a second time for a brisk walk around town — a run, in fact. She passed Chad the MC, who flagged her down. He had been walking with Bob and his pregnant live-in; the two moseyed on up ahead so as not to appear obtrusive, peering back at Chad and Nance nonetheless.

"Did you find the necklace?" the MC said.

Nance shook her head.

"She's been looking for that necklace every summer that I can remember."

Nance saw from the lines around Chad's eyes that he was older than she'd thought, possibly older than herself. "Would you like to go have a drink?" she heard herself say.

"Up there's a good place." He indicated an old, fixed-up hotel she'd passed earlier, on a steep hill, tables on the front porch overlooking the harbor.

■ Later they ran back to the ship holding hands in a drizzle that threatened to become more. It was late afternoon and the clouds were so dark that the boat had turned on all its lights. Abruptly Chad let go of her hand. She understood: he didn't want anyone to see them. Neither did she. He wasn't her type, he had the manner of a game-show host, she disliked his blond looks — and she couldn't keep away from him. There were endless reasons to avoid him. And she wouldn't — just like a heroine in one of Ellie's trashy books. "Inexplicably drawn to him, and knowing they could never be together but for this one moment, she allowed him to bury his head in her bosom." Wasn't this an exact quotation?

She'd had the feeling, when she and Chad were holding hands, that Ellie was watching. Smacking her lips, as she tended to do when reading a particularly riveting passage. Maybe she'd spent the past several summers trying to set someone up with Chad — Nance's sister or one of the cousins — a project as consuming, and as futile, as finding a necklace to match her dead sister's earrings.

Once on board, Nance half expected Ellie to be waiting for her, clanking her cane against the ship's hull. No. She checked Ellie's room: no light under the door. Knocking softly, she entered. Ellie was asleep, snoring, book on her chest. Nance backed out of the room, only to hear Ellie stir. "Is that you? Sally?"

"It's Nance. Go back to sleep."

Ellie switched on the light. "Why, you're soaking wet!"

"Well — " Nance wasn't exactly soaking, her clothes were damp, that was all, but there was no point in arguing. "I had a drink with Chad, up at that old hotel." She offered this as a distraction, a sort of payment or trade in kind.

"A drink?" Ellie set down her book eagerly. On the cover was a hula girl, grass skirt low on her hips, the standard cleavage, a man nuzzling her neck. "Is he your beau?"

"What?" Nance heard the old-fashioned word as *bow*: a ribbon tied gaudily, a birthday present, a wedding present.

"Beau. Your boyfriend." Ellie smacked her lips.

"My God, Ellie, we just had a drink." So it was true: Ellie had a dirty mind. An odd term. Nance imagined the whiskey sours she and Chad had drunk — but filled with dirty dishwater, brown and sudsy, bobbing with sludge and the remains of food. How his hand had traveled up her thigh, after playing footsy under the table. *How tacky,* she'd thought with a surge of excitement. *Isn't this just like him?* She swatted his hand away, a little late.

They'd been talking about sex. How it could be unsatisfactory with a loved one — someone you were living with, say (his situation), or (her situation) someone you once loved but for whom you now felt only respect. "Sex," she'd heard herself say, "is something we politely do for each other." She'd made her relationship sound like more than it was; what it really amounted to was going to the movies once a week, sleeping together afterward, the release of orgasm to get her through another uneventful week. But to Chad she'd used words like *fiancé* and *engagement* — to counteract the unhappy information that Chad was so seriously involved. His significant other, he called her.

She giggled. "I thought you said 'subsequent other.'"

He had his fingers practically at her groin. "No, she's pretty significant," he whispered in her ear, "in that I haven't known how to get away from her. Until I met you."

Liar, she thought now. As if she were one to talk. Fortunately, Ellie seemed to have forgotten Chad and was rattling on about the rain, the food. She handed Nance an envelope. "You'll need this," she said.

Nance knew what was inside. The only question was how much.

"Buy yourself a sweater. Something warm. You're drenched, like they all get. Buy yourself a dress, there's a dance tonight. Wait till this storm passes over, and while you're out, get me a new book, will you? This one's a bore, thoroughly predictable."

■ So Nance went to town for the third time. In the same boutique where she bought the dress, amazingly, she found a necklace to match the earrings — it was a secondhand store, the classy kind, antique clothes and jewelry. Not a store Ellie would frequent. The necklace wasn't an exact match, but a close one: a string of white porcelain globes beaded together with bits of brass. Nance would offer to paint on the pink flowers; she knew how to do such projects, in charge of window displays for Simpleman's, often hired by clients to do lettering, graphics, small art jobs.

The necklace she paid for with her own money; she didn't buy a sweater.

At a corner drugstore she bought Ellie a book, *Love's Remains,* a picture of a fleshy woman on the cover, bodice unbuttoned, a man somewhere behind her. On none of the books' covers, Nance noticed, did a woman stand alone, nor was she ever anything less than a D-cup.

Wearing the new dress back to the ship, she appreciated the air on her skin, cool and moist; the dress's pale yellow sash crisscrossed her exposed back, chafing her like a medieval corset — a sensation she liked also.

On board she fell in with a line of elderly passengers attired as though going to church — coats and ties, furs and wraps, the men freshly shaved, the women smelling of Estée Lauder — en route to the dining room, where the dance would be held.

Nance stopped at Ellie's door and knocked. "Are you ready to go to the dance, Ellie?"

"I am. Just putting on my lipstick. Come in!"

In the same blue silk dress and brooch, she was applying a thick red lipstick that for some reason filled Nance with despair. The book with the hula girl lay face down on the bed. "Oh!" Nance said. "I nearly forgot. Here's a new book, and this." She handed the bag with the necklace to Ellie, who reached inside.

"My word, where did you find this? Get my purse! I want to see if they match."

"They don't, Ellie, not perfectly." She didn't know which purse, so she got both. It took Ellie several minutes to find the coin purse with the earrings, then to unwrap the tissue paper.

"I can paint on the flowers," Nance said, "every other bead, I was thinking. So it's not overkill."

Ellie seemed uninterested in the details. "Where did you find it?" she said. "I've been looking for years."

"A place that sells antique jewelry and clothes." She didn't want to say secondhand store. "I bought this dress there, too." Ellie, so far, hadn't noticed the dress — irritating. Nance couldn't bring herself to say thank you, even though Ellie's money had bought the dress. As she pivoted so Ellie could see, she glimpsed her back, strafed with yellow sash, in the mirror. A character in one of Ellie's books might wear this dress, except it would be turned around backward, sashes barely containing breasts that threatened to spill out everywhere. A tarty, buxom character — not the heroine, but her well-meaning friend with a heart of gold, who also lacked taste and morals.

"It becomes you," was all that Ellie said, then went back to admiring the necklace; Nance couldn't tell if this was a compliment or not.

■ In the dining room only one couple was dancing, Bob and his pregnant live-in, when Nance and Ellie entered. The other passengers sat at tables and, dressed in all their finery, gnawed on chicken wings.

"Last year they served spaghetti and meatballs," Ellie said, "which was worse. Everybody spotted their clothes. Wouldn't you think the staff would catch on by now?"

She stopped the maitre d' on his rounds; to complain about the chicken, Nance thought. No. To slip him a five-dollar bill. "Wonderful meal," she said. "Lovely party."

Bob and his live-in performed another solitary sweaty dance: a cross between a tango and some kind of bump and grind routine — difficult to accomplish with such a large belly between them.

"Bravo, bravo!" cried Ellie, reaching into her purse for another five. Was she going to tip *them?*

Then Nance saw Chad making his way toward her from across the room, swinging his mike — this one had a cord — around and around while sashaying his hips — God. Couldn't the man act normal? She escaped to the bar, but he caught up with her.

"You look like a milkmaid in that dress — a naughty one." He held out an arm to her, mock debonair. "Dance?"

"Maybe. Once I finish my drink." She noticed Ellie watching them.

Out on the dance floor, Chad spun her around expertly, first a jitterbug, then the cha-cha. "I'm a pro," he acknowledged. "I have to be, to dance with all the old ladies. They think I'm sweet. Their husbands can't, or won't."

She pictured his hand on their girdled hips and for the moment felt no attraction to him, relievedly so. Two or three couples joined them — those husbands willing, she supposed, and able, foxtrotting their wives across the room. Chad danced her into the kitchen, while over his shoulder Nance looked for Ellie, not seeing her — probably busy handing out fives to the staff. "Come on," Chad said, "I want to show you something." He led her to a walk-in cooler, where he poured her a glass of champagne.

"Trying to get me drunk again," she said, and he was. He was that obvious.

"I have something even better, are you ready?" He brought her inside the cooler and shut the door, made her close her eyes. "You can open them now," he said.

An entire shelf filled with cans of whipped cream.

"Ah," he said, "cream for the milkmaid."

Nance rolled her eyes — was this supposed to get her in the mood?

He lifted one can, popped the top off, opened his mouth and inserted the nozzle. "Nitrous oxide," he said. "Want some?"

She almost laughed it was so absurd. He pressed the nozzle, inhaled, held his breath, then said in a squeaky voice, "This is what we do for fun around here, once the passengers go to bed. It's amazing the chef can get these things to squirt any cream — no propellent left."

"Well, it's not bedtime yet. Aren't you worried we'll be caught?"

"Nobody's around," he said. He sang: "Dessert's on the table, dinner's over . . . "

She realized she hadn't eaten, that she wasn't at all hungry.

"Besides," Chad said, "I'd just explain I'm getting my milkmaid a little cream. What could be more innocent?" He draped his arm around her bare shoulder, tickling the nozzle against her lips. "Come on, baby. Open up for Daddy. Time for your bottle."

Automatically she opened her mouth — some kind of instinct left over from infancy. There was a whoosh. "Hold your breath," he said.

She pictured whipped cream on pie, on cake, on blackberries; she pictured people skiing. She thought of that woman on the cover of the old Tijuana Brass album, voluptuous in her dress of whipped cream — she'd read somewhere that it was really shaving cream.

She felt nothing. "Maybe it doesn't work on me."

He had her try it again and again, until she felt giddy — the nitrous oxide, or was she just hyperventilating? Her fingers went numb, her scalp tingled. Chad had his hand down the bodice of her dress. He loosened the sash, scooped both hands inside; he pressed up against her, she pressed back and listened to herself make soft moaning noises. Chad busied himself untying the sash altogether—it had gotten into knots. As you would undo the strings on a roast before you ate it, she thought. Of course those you would snip with scissors. He turned her back around and sank his blond head to her chest. "I love you, I love you," he said. She felt ridiculous, unable to stop. A juvenile excitement, like making out in the back of a car. That she might have sex with him right here in the cooler, with someone likely to walk in any minute; that she might become pregnant or catch a disease. That she couldn't reverse things now—this made her want him more. He maneuvered her to the floor, cold rubber mats and the smell of celery sticks, cream cheese, a smell that wouldn't go away, and as deftly as he danced old ladies across a room, he had gotten up her skirt, slipped off her underwear.

■ Later she knocked on Ellie's door.

"Yes? Come in." Though it was nighttime, Ellie had arranged herself near the porthole as usual, the new book in her lap.

"Just checking up on you. I didn't know where you'd gone."

"Nor me you. Though I had an idea."

Nance chose to ignore this. "Can I get you anything?" She smoothed her dress, aware suddenly that it hung crookedly—she'd missed a loop with her sash.

"Nothing, thank you." Ellie set her book down. "How old are you, Nance?"

A rarity: Ellie in the mood to talk. Nance pictured Chad pacing near her stateroom door, trying not to be so obvious as to stand right by it. She'd told him to meet her there, a test, she realized now—to see if he loved her. Crazily, alarmingly, it seemed possible he did. A test to see if she loved him. Of course she didn't.

"I'm thirty, Ellie."

"Not married."

"You know I'm not."

"By your age I was."

"I know, and you had two children." Trying to speed her along; she'd heard this before.

"Two little stinkers. No time for fun," Ellie said, "with two little stinkers."

It was family lore: Ellie and her two little stinkers, the children she could scarcely manage, raising them akin to raising the Titanic.

"No time for anything but wiping their little bottoms and keeping them from killing each other. Whew! Once we got away. A train trip to Manitoba, don't ask me why we went there."

This part was new.

"My husband couldn't go, so it was the two of us."

Who was 'us'? She didn't ask, hoping Ellie would get to the point. She'd never met Ellie's husband. To her knowledge, nobody in the family had. It was believed they'd divorced somewhere along the line, although Ellie never said.

"We got a sleeper car. Bunks right on top of each other."

"Who?" Nance asked finally, exasperated. It was her own fault — why had she stopped by? Habit, or to cover her bases, give herself an alibi: *The dance? I missed most of it, wanted to check on Ellie, she gets lonely even if she won't admit it.* A pretty lame alibi, even it was true; everybody had seen her dancing with Chad, had seen her leave with him and come back later, her dress on crooked. And what did she care anyway?

"Who?" Ellie said. "My sister. Ten years younger than me. She lived with us, you know."

"Hmm." Nance had hoped it would be a lover. Knowing it wouldn't. Then she realized. "Your sister? That sister?"

She saw the earrings on the bedside table, arranged with the necklace.

"Stupid girl." Ellie pressed her lips together, waxy flakes of lipstick flecking her chin. "Do you know what that stupid girl did? It was during the day and she was sitting by the window — " Ellie raised her eyes to the ceiling, apparently collecting her thoughts. Nance imagined the story she would tell: her sister meeting a man on the train — a salesman, a soldier, a mason — becoming pregnant, settling in some prairie town. Dying later on, in childbirth or after a long life filled with dust and disappointment.

"It was so hot she opened the window. No air conditioning in those days. And then we passed the buffalo, everywhere there were buffalo. As if we were in the last century, you could imagine men hunting them out the windows of the train. For no reason! Shooting! Leaving the carcasses to rot. Sally must've had the same thought. Why were there all these buffalo—weren't they all dead like we'd heard? She stuck her head out the window and began yelling 'Stop! Stop!'—I don't know why, she was prone to that sort of thing. Passionate, an animal lover, a tendency to go wild. But I would've done the same if I had been sitting there. Would've stuck *my* head out the window. Then whoosh, the other train comes along and she was gone."

"What?" Nance said.

"It decapitated her, dear."

"What?" Nance sat down on Ellie's bed, from the shock. "What did you do?"

"What was there to do?"

Nance meant the blood, surely there had to be a lot of blood, and where was the sister's head? She meant exactly what she had said: what did you do? Scream, call for help? What did you do with what was left of her? Had Ellie been helped from the room? Were there other witnesses? Did the train stop or keep going?

She glanced at the earrings on the bedside table, rolling slightly with the sway of the boat. Unbidden, the image of Chad's baby-smooth chest rising and falling, on top of her. She wondered if Ellie's story were true; why hadn't she heard it before?

"I'm sorry, Ellie. I'm terribly sorry." She took Ellie's hand. Ellie drew it away.

"She was a stupid girl. Stupid for doing that."

"Don't blame yourself, Ellie. There was nothing you could do." She patted the old woman's shoulder, then let her hand remain there. Both of them stared at it briefly, the hand appearing stiff and unnatural, like a fish from the market perched on Ellie's shoulder.

"I feel just awful," Nance continued. "Isn't there something I can do for you? Is there something you would like? Hot tea? A blanket?"

Never had she felt so awkward at comforting someone, but that was just the thing: Ellie seemed to require no comforting. Disliked it, in fact, disliked *her*. Even if the story weren't true—though Nance felt that it was—it occurred to her that she might not be the first to hear it; that her sister or cousins might've heard exactly the same revelation, at exactly the same point. The night of the dance, on their way to or from a tryst with someone they hardly knew. Chad, perhaps. "Does anyone else know?" Nance asked. "I thought—maybe because of the necklace, now that you have a match—I thought maybe you hadn't told anyone."

"You aren't privy to a great secret," Ellie said, "if that's what you mean. You can go now. Go on to your beau."

"Ellie! I wouldn't think of leaving now. After what you told me?"

"Go to your beau. Fool! Ninny!"

"Chad is not my beau."

I am not foolish, she wanted to add, or blind. Her eyes were wide open, she expected nothing. Who was Ellie to be lecturing her? Ellie with her books and her divorce and her children who eschewed her. Did anyone in this world truly love Ellie? Did anyone love her—Nance?

"Please, Ellie. I'd like to stay. I'll get you some tea." She felt she ought to be kind to her, loving—the loss of a sister, no matter how many years ago.

But Ellie would have none of her kindness. She picked up her book and resumed reading, as though Nance weren't there at all, the purpose and timing of her revelation known only to her, leaving Nance to hover in the doorway saying, "Ellie? Ellie!"

■ She waited at the railing just outside her room. He wouldn't show up; there was nothing enduring about Chad.

"You are beautiful," he had said to her afterward. As she stood there, her dress and its ungainly long sash gathered up around her chest. "You are beautiful." As if she were something he wasn't able to pass up. A dessert. A bit of scenery for one's enjoyment. *The San Juans are beautiful.* They were: foggy, green, hilly, mysterious, the boat gliding along.

She was not.

She leaned over the railing. There seemed to be something floating, something white and fleshy; she couldn't make it out in the dark. An albino fish, a piece of styrofoam, a discarded cast from an arm or leg; it drifted by, then was gone.

The night was clear and silent; islands passed by, ghostly dark humps of animals hunted to extinction. At last she went to her room, not bothering with the lights. She didn't see him at first, naked in her bed, eyes open, the thief, the poacher.

POLAROID

Mom's just announced the next stop in our family vacation: Solvang. Only twenty miles to go. She reads aloud from the guidebook, "Who would ever expect to find a Danish village in the middle of the California countryside?"

I don't know what's so surprising about it, we've been coming here every year since I can remember. Every year Mom, Dad, Chuck, and I drive all over the state for two weeks gawking at redwoods and the Golden Gate Bridge, oohing and ahhing over Hearst Castle, feeding the bears at Yosemite. You probably think I'm kidding about the bears. Nope. We drive somewhere scenic, like the Yosemite municipal dump, throw the remains of our picnic lunch out the windows, roll 'em up, and here come the bears. "Aren't they sweet?" my mother always says till I want to scream. There is nothing *sweet* about overweight bears at a dump eating people's leftover food. But I never scream at her, I never scream at anyone. I talk in a low calm voice, especially to my mother, who gets excited easily. Right now she's going on and on about Solvang as if we'd never been there before. "You know," she says, "of all the places in the whole world, Solvang is my very favorite." My mother's never been out of the state of California.

As for Solvang, it's this place with diesel-powered windmills and smorgasbords and at least six pastry shops per block. If not pastry, fudge — and as any intelligent person knows, fudge is not Danish. It's about as Danish as the "natives" themselves, pink-cheeked and blond, probably full-blooded natives of Redondo Beach; the women in crinoline petticoats, the men in lederhosen — aren't lederhosen Swiss? — and everybody stomping around in clogs. There's not one thing Danish about Solvang, but try telling my parents that. They'd never believe you, and besides, Solvang's as close as they'll ever get to Denmark.

Meet my family, the Greenes. My mother and father could be twins. She's the one with the bow in her hair, he's the one driving. Both are big and I mean fat, both are wearing shirts that say WE'RE FROM DISNEYLAND, ANAHEIM, CALIFORNIA. Mom got the shirts especially for this trip. She says they identify us as a family, but I refuse to wear mine. No way I'd wear a shirt like that; it even has a picture of the Matterhorn on the front. We almost had a fight about it with Mom saying what's the matter with me, didn't I have a sense of humor, and besides, we should be proud of where we're from, Disneyland being of international fame. Right up there, Mom, with Rome and Washington, D.C., Paris. Of course I'd never *say* such a thing. All I said was I preferred not to wear the shirt, thank you.

Chuck's crazy about his shirt. He's six years younger than me and doesn't know any better — I just turned eighteen. Chuck. Chubby Chuck. Have you ever seen pinker skin or more dimples? Right now he's blowing his nose. Allergies. There's wads of wet squishy Kleenex all over the back seat and I think, get me out of this car. The air conditioner's going full blast, the windows are rolled up. It smells in here of Oreos and orange soda and fat people, I can't breathe. Get me away from these people, I'm not related to them.

Look at them, look at me. I'm bones all over; you couldn't find their bones if you tried, certainly not Mom's. Under that extra-extra-large jumbo Disneyland T-shirt there's a gigantic happy pastry puff, a pastry face with nose and eyes ... Yes, we have the same color eyes but big deal! Any fool could see I'm adopted. Look at Chuck, dimples where his knuckles ought to be. He's their real kid, I'm not. I was born out of wedlock somewhere and handed over to them in a blanket. "You're my very own," Mom said once and showed me her stretch marks.

Disgusting.

I remember her chasing me around with the vacuum cleaner one time — it was a little game we used to play — when I just looked at her and ran under a bed screaming I didn't want to play anymore. I was afraid she would suck me up inside her and in my childish way I knew that's what she wanted, to make me a part of her. But something wasn't right. I *wasn't* a part of her, I didn't belong to her, she was just borrowing me for a while. All this I tried to tell her from underneath the bed, until finally she pulled me out and held me. Even then I was stiff in her arms, afraid of getting lost or swallowed up.

She's still trying to make me a part of her, a part of them. "Our last trip together as a family," she's said every day now for the last week. What she means is, I'm leaving for college in a month. College in another state, clear across the country, college in a nice big dirty city, far, far away. Among, as Mom puts it, perfect strangers. That's what I'm looking forward to the most — perfect strangers.

I can tell Mom's pretty upset about my going away. All during the trip she's been churning out picture after picture on the Polaroid: me next to Dad, me next to Chuck and Dad, me and Chuck, Mom and me. Then the whole family together, usually taken by some Japanese tourist with glasses; then Dad takes a picture of him and his wife on their camera, and they rush off to catch up with their tour group, led by some guy carrying a red flag. No matter who takes the picture, though, you can count on Mom to make sure I'm in it. She's literally been trailing me with that camera, even though I've begged her not to. But every time I turn around it's "Smile, Melissa, smile!" Posed shots, candid shots, terrible shots one and all.

Then, every night at dinner, Mom goes over the day's batch of pictures. Remember that game, what's wrong with the picture? That's me, I'm the part that's wrong with the picture, the part that doesn't fit. Especially in the group shots. I look like a tall skinny lamp standing next to a bunch of grinning overstuffed chairs.

Mom thinks I'm too skinny. She's all worried I'll get that disease, anorexia nervosa, as if it's something you *catch*. Just because I'm not built like a couch, just because I believe in a little exercise now and then.

That's what I can't stand about these trips — we never get out of the car. Or if we do, it's only long enough to stretch our legs and eat a great big meal or snack. This must be Mom's way of fattening me up — making me sit in a car all day, letting me out only to eat.

You want to know the real reason my family likes Solvang so much? The reason they wouldn't miss it for the world? The food. That's all there is to do in Solvang. Eat.

■ We've been in Solvang five or ten minutes now, but we're still riding around in the car with the windows rolled up. Dad claims he's looking for a place to park, but every time I point one out he says no, no, no, let's park up close so we don't have to walk so far. And besides, we've got *all* afternoon, so why not take our time, drive around a bit, get the feel of the place.

"That's true," Mom says, a map in front of her face. "What's the rush?"

It's obvious she's not in any rush — she's had that map in front of her face ever since we got here. As for Chuck, he doesn't even know he's in a car; he's sound asleep.

I glance over Mom's shoulder at the map. It's a map of Solvang left over from last year's trip, and at the top it says SO MUCH TO SEE AND DO. What, I would like to know, exactly *what* is there to do or see here? So far Solvang looks the same as it did last year and the year before that, like an advertisement for Kodak. Packed with tourists, but clean. Too clean, as if they hose everything down at night — the sidewalks, the buildings, the windmills, the tulips, even the sky.

Now Mom's gabbing away about what we're going to do for the next three hours, which basically boils down to what and where to eat, with maybe a little shopping thrown in. Shopping for what I have no idea — it's all junk — unless you prefer to delude yourself that what you buy here is made in Denmark rather than Korea, Taiwan, or Mexico.

Then, right in the middle of Mom's itinerary, Dad begins to sing: "The bluest skies you'll ever see are in Seattle ... " He has a habit of singing on these trips, and in fact his favorite car game is Guess That Tune, except the only songs he knows are old TV songs. "The greenest trees you'll ever see are in Seattle ... "

"Here Come the Brides," I say, hoping he'll take a hint. Because once he gets a song on the brain we have to hear it all day long. Yesterday it was "Cousins, identical cousins all the way ... " "Patty Duke," I said. "Patty Duke!" I kept on saying. I must've said "Patty Duke" two dozen times.

"Like a hope, a little child, running free, running wild ... "

"Dad, I said Here Come the Brides."

"Da da da-da da-da da, da da da-da da-da da ... "

"Please." It's no use, he's having the time of his life. I see some parking spaces up on the left. "We could park there," I say as we glide right past them. We're on the outskirts of town, I should've remembered. Too far to walk.

"Da da da-da da-da da, da da da-da da-da da ... "

"Please can't we park." I'm actually whining. This is torture. How have I stood it this long? Only a few more days, I tell myself; you are patient, you are eighteen years old. But I can't take another day of this trip. If I die and go to hell it will be like this: stuck in a car with my family, driving around Solvang at five miles an hour, the windows rolled up, the doors locked. Dad will sing TV songs as Mom reads aloud from a guidebook, and Chuck will blow his nose, and everyone will eat from a bottomless bag of Oreos.

Dad swings around a corner too sharp, sending Chuck into my lap. He doesn't even wake up, probably exhausted from all the sugar he's eaten today. I look at his open mouth. It's all pink inside, no teeth showing. Like a baby's mouth, ugly. I whisper, "Time to wake up, Chuck, time to eat. Want another cookie?" I stop myself, what am I saying? Being cooped up in a car must do this to you — make you regress. Chuck could be two, I could be eight. We could be playing the game I called Mean Mother. I would croon motherly words at him, only in a mean voice. "Eat your oatmeal, Chuck." "Don't you want to go out and play?" "Your hair needs brushing." Chuck would listen with wide eyes, then he'd start to cry; I liked it. And now, right now, I can feel that same nastiness welling up inside me. It needs an outlet. *I* need an outlet — I need to get out of this car.

But no, we're at a stoplight now, waiting for people to cross. "Park the car, Dad, park the car," I chant under my breath. "Park the car, Dad, park the car." Chuck stirs in my lap. He sits up, lets loose a big wet sniffle, grabs for a Kleenex. "Park the car, Dad, park the car." The crosswalk is swarming with tourists gawking at the street signs written in Danish, clutching cameras and ham sandwiches. "Park the car, park the car."

As we wait and wait and wait and wait for the light to change, Dad starts in with the Here Come the Brides again, only this time he's whistling. Meanwhile Mom recites a moment by moment account of last year's trip to Solvang. "Then we had lunch at that smorgasbord, remember? Oh, the *casseroles,* but dessert was the best. Danish pastry pie."

"A hot dog," Chuck says, "I want a hot dog."

Dad's whistling, Mom's talking — they don't even hear him. "Can I have a hot dog?" He's practically whining in my ear. "I want a hot dog, they better have hot dogs here."

At last, a green light. Dad eases the car down the street; I could crawl faster than this.

"I want a hot dog."

"Shut up." I rock back and forth in my seat, as if this will make the car go faster.

"If they have hot dogs, can I have a hot dog?"

Mom turns around in her seat. "What?" But she's not paying attention to Chuck; no, she's aiming the Polaroid at me.

"A hot dog, I want a —"

"No more hot dogs," I snarl at the camera. The shutter clicks.

"Candid camera!" Mom says. Then to me, "What did you say?"

"Nothing, nothing."

Relief in sight: Dad is pulling into a parking space.

■ An hour out of Solvang and already we're stopped at a restaurant for—what else—an early dinner before we turn in for a night of TV watching and cookie eating at the Motel 6. So here we are, crammed into a booth at the Black Oak Coffee Shop, sharing one dinky little menu. Other than the herd of RVs in the parking lot, there's not much in the way of scenery here. Just a lot of grassy hills and, I might add, not a tree in sight, much less an oak tree.

When the waitress finally gets around to our table, both Mom and Dad order the lasagna special, while Chuck—happy, lucky Chuck—opts for hot dogs and french fries. Despite Mom's prodding, all I order is soup and crackers. Thanks to this afternoon, it's all I can stomach.

Of course, having to look at Chuck and Dad from the necks up isn't exactly soothing my stomach any. Both have on these Tyrolean hats they bought in Solvang, feathers in the brim, the whole bit. But that's nothing compared to what *I've* got on. I'm wearing this bright yellow dress with big puffy sleeves and a full skirt, complete with embroidered flowers on the pockets and a mile—and I mean a mile—of white rick-rack. I look like birthday cake. This dress, this monstrosity, is the whole reason Mom wanted to go shopping in Solvang. It turns out she's waited an entire year to get me this dress, this very dress. And even though she bought the dress for me, I think of it as my gift for her.

Our food arrives and everybody's about to dig in when Mom reaches into her straw bag for today's batch of pictures. She lays them out on the table, then acts puzzled; she's checking her bag, sorting through the pictures in front of her. "Where is it?" she says.

"Where's what?" says Dad, spooning lasagna into his mouth.

"The picture of Melissa, the one I took in the car."

"It's a terrible picture," I say, and it is. The worst. Still, I remember Mom saying how much she liked that picture and why: she thinks I'm smiling, when actually I'm glaring into the camera, my teeth bared.

But there's no convincing Mom. She wants to run out to the car and check. "It will just take a minute," she says. "I'm sure I left it on the front seat." Dad tells her to relax and eat her dinner; he passes her the salt. It's obvious he doesn't understand this sudden fixation of hers any more than I do. Mom dumps the usual amount of salt on her food, but I can tell she's distracted. She really wants that picture. Then she's reaching into her bag again, this time for the Polaroid. She's got a better idea, she says, in honor of my new dress: she'll take another picture of me here, right here in the restaurant. "We can watch it develop while we eat!" she says.

And before I can refuse or talk her out of it, she's on her feet, waving her enormous arms at Chuck and Dad, ordering them to scoot over, scoot over, out of the way. I look to Dad for help; he shrugs and takes his plate with him. Mom pauses to wipe her hands on her shirt, her Disneyland shirt. "Now," she says, raising the camera to her face.

I'm all ready with my best smile so we can get this over with, when she says in the loudest voice you ever heard, "Cheese! Cheese!"

Everybody in the restaurant stops cold, including the chef who pokes his head out to see what's going on, and I'm not sure what I'm doing — if I'm smiling or not — when Mom snaps the picture.

Then I hear the applause. *Applause.* Why are these people clapping? Do they think it's my birthday? What bothers me most, though, is the sound of their clapping. It hurts my ears, as if I'm being slapped and hit — more like punishment than praise.

Mom slides into the booth next to Dad. She's radiant. She sets the picture on the table and we watch as it develops. The picture goes from gray to a kind of orange, then we see shapes — the shape of my head, the outline of my body. The colors get brighter, but they're the wrong colors. My dress is more green than yellow, and my face is chalk white. I am smiling, only I look terrified, as if somebody's holding a gun to my head.

"Ugly," Chuck says.

He's right. The picture could not be uglier. Still, Mom loves it; she's all but cradling it in her arms. Then she tries to force it into her wallet, in with my grammar school shots. It's too wide, the picture won't fit. Her eyes are red—is she crying? I know I should do something, tell her I'm not leaving for good, that I'll come back on vacations. Hug her. Something. But I can't seem to move or talk.

Mom's pretending not to cry and we're all pretending not to notice. She takes a bite of her lasagna and chews and puts her fork down and says with her mouth full, "You're my baby."

I can't even look at her. When I was younger I believed my real parents were dark and handsome foreigners who had to leave the country and, for mysterious reasons, couldn't take me with them. So they left me with these people, in the care of this big waddling woman who somehow got it in her head that she was my mother. She fed and clothed me and enrolled me in Brownies and Girl Scouts and clapped over every miserable little thing I did.

She's still crying, quietly weeping into her lasagna. Without thinking I push my glass of water to her side of the table.

Of all the things I could do for her, I give her water.

She takes a sip, even though she has her own glass. Dad looks uncomfortable, embarrassed. Chuck pushes the french fries around his plate and suddenly I'm starving, hungry and thirsty all at the same time. The soup and crackers aren't enough. I want more. I try to think what it is I want, all the food I could order here. Lasagna, fried chicken, mashed potatoes, pie; I could have pie. But nothing sounds good, nothing tastes good. Nothing will go down my throat.

REGIONS OF THE EARTH

It wasn't until they moved in that they discovered neighbors — in the basement. There existed in the basement of the house Paul and Maxine Baber had rented another entire two-bedroom apartment containing an entire family, a husband and a wife and two children, a little girl and an infant.

"How could we not have noticed?" Paul said to Maxine.

"Why didn't Ed tell us?" Ed was the dentist-landlord, who rapidly in Maxine's mind was becoming not Ed any longer, but just the landlord.

The neighbors' baby was crying, screeching. Maxine turned up the radio. There was a knock on the door. Maxine opened it. "Yes?"

"I'm from downstairs and I was wondering ..."

Maxine didn't respond.

"The baby." The anemically pale woman twisted her hands. "The baby's trying to sleep, and I thought maybe you could turn your radio down? And maybe move it? It's right over the baby's room."

"Sure," Maxine said.

"No problem," Paul added from across the room. "I'm Paul, by the way, and this is my wife, Maxine."

Maxine thought the woman might introduce herself, say perhaps, "So how's it going, you getting settled and all?" or "Ed tells me you just got married." Or "Sorry about the radio, you know how babies are." Instead the woman glanced just behind her, up into the branches of their jointly shared crab apple tree, blossoms lost, now spiked with leaves; her thin, freckled arm gestured uselessly. "Already hot," she said, "and it's only May."

The baby was shrieking louder and louder. Maxine could not only hear but actually feel it crying — the floorboards vibrated, the walls echoed with the sound. The woman looked at them as if helpless, as if they, the Babers, might be able to do something. "That's my son," she said, and left.

■ Due to an arrangement with the previous tenants, which the landlord had also neglected to mention to the Babers, the couple in the basement kept their washer and dryer in the upstairs apartment because they didn't have hookups. This meant that the woman, Ann, brought up baskets of laundry to do whenever she felt like it — usually when Paul and Maxine were just settling down to work at their respective computers, or when they were about to make love; their bedroom was right off the kitchen.

Once they accidentally left the bedroom door open — this was, after all, their apartment, supposedly nobody there but them, the newlyweds — only to be interrupted by Ann lugging in, with a sigh, an overflowing laundry basket. Paul slammed the door. "Oh," they heard her say, followed by the click of the back door, the sound of Ann shuffling back down the steps. By then they'd lost the mood anyway, so they relented, went downstairs and banged on the door. "Ann? It's okay now! You can do the laundry!"

So that afternoon, like most, they listened to the dryer squeak and felt the kitchen, the whole house, fill with hot, linty air while Ann went up and down the steps, crying baby on her hip, her five-year-old running all over the yard yelling in the Baber's windows, looking for her mother: "MOMMY!"

When the baby wasn't on her hip, Ann would stand in the Babers' kitchen making monotonous small talk if, say, Paul or Maxine happened to go in there for a glass of water or a peach: "It sure is hot. We went to the church today and somebody passed out."

■ Paul had the summer off in order to finish his dissertation. Maxine, meanwhile, had her thesis to finish, which she was scheduled to defend in the fall.

They worked at opposite ends of the house, Paul in one of the bedrooms — really a converted pantry — with a shelf by the door that caused him to bump his head whenever he went by, and Maxine in the damp front room that, she told herself, was cool if mildewy. It was also the room they stored things in — wedding presents, boxes they hadn't gotten around to unpacking, each other's furniture they couldn't tolerate but hadn't the heart or the guts to throw away.

Maxine worked not at a desk but on an old door across two sawhorses, the area around her feet thick with books, notes, abandoned paragraphs — stray sheets from the printer. She couldn't complete anything. She'd begin the concluding chapter, only to switch over to revising chapter three, only to drift off and stare out the window, listening for the phone to ring, for the mailman's step on the porch — anything to break the tedium. She wondered about being married. Here she was, married. Everyone seemed to think it so normal, but she'd never thought it would happen to her. She still couldn't believe it and would look at the gold band often, watching it instead of her thesis as her fingers moved across the keyboard.

All she could think about, too, was getting pregnant, although they'd decided to wait a year. At least. But she had to check her actions and double-check — making sure the amount of jelly in the diaphragm was correct, making sure she put the jelly in at all. Twice now they'd skipped the diaphragm altogether. Their lovemaking was ecstatic, so biological, as if they meant to fill out the thinly populated regions of the earth.

Though she supposed she wanted, unconsciously at least, to get pregnant, Maxine had not much affinity for children. Especially Ann's five-year-old. "My name is Joe-za-*phine*," the girl had told her. "And you better say it right." She had said this while standing outside the window of Maxine's office; had come up to the window for no other reason than to say her name and flounce off.

Maxine had made the mistake of laughing. A mistake because from that day on, Josephine would appear at her window. Or Paul's. She spent her mornings going from window to window searching for one of the Babers. "Mrs. Baber? Is that you? MRS. BABER!" Once she knew you were there and listening, she'd perform for you — throwing her doll into her play pool and screaming Jesus songs at it.

Maxine had tried to have a little talk with her, on the front steps of the house. "Now Josephine," she said, "even though Paul and I don't go to an office, we work. We can't be disturbed. Of course you can play in your pool and sing, or whatever you want to do, but please don't call our names. We can't get our work done that way. Do you understand?"

"Uh-huh," Josephine said, her gaze on the screen door. Paul was emerging from his office. "Is that Mr. Baber?"

"You can call us by our first names, Josephine, if you like. I'm Maxine and that's Paul."

"Where is Mr. Baber going?" She sounded nearly heartbroken.

"Just to the bathroom, I think. He'll be back, don't worry. Now, Josephine, what did I say about calling out our names while we work?"

"I know," she said.

But it didn't stop. Maxine moved to the extreme corner of her work table, where Josephine couldn't see her; Paul pulled the shade in his office. They considered talking to Ann but held off. Josephine, they conjectured, would grow out of this — it was merely the stress of having a new baby brother, the sudden loss of attention. And the poor child had no friends her own age. Ann never took her anywhere, never had anyone over.

So they tried ignoring Josephine, pretending not to see her at the windows, her little chin propped on the sill. "What are you doing, Mr.

Baber? Where's Mrs. Baber?" At times they had to sneak from room to room—say, into the bedroom to retrieve a book—shinnying along the wall like burglars, because they could hear Josephine out there doing her rounds, going window to window in the endless and fascinating search for Mr. and Mrs. Baber.

■ Maxine needed total quiet in order to work.

Paul, on the other hand, liked to boast he could work under any conditions—in gloomy basements, cars, buses, phones ringing, people shouting, too hot, too cold, construction going on. Nothing impaired his concentration. But that summer he was getting little work done either. "It's the pressure," he said. "The *having* to get it done. They gave me the summer off. I have to get this done! Why can't I work? Why can't I settle down?"

Instead of working, they obsessed about the things that needed repairing: a ceiling fan that didn't work, ripped and ill-fitting screens that let in a horde of moths every night, and a tub that, whenever you took a bath, leaked into the basement bathroom: the water actually poured down the walls. And the fact that there was only one outlet in the kitchen—one!—so that in order to toast bread, they had to set the toaster on the washer, not to mention the coffee pot and the radio, all of which Ann would efficiently set aside, right on top of the dirty dishes by the sink, each time she had a basketful of dirty clothes, which was daily, hourly.

They called the landlord, only to get his answering machine. "Say Ed, this is Paul Baber, you know, on Pine Street. We've got a problem we'd like you to fix . . ." A week after such calls, Ed would finally drop by unannounced, loudly bang around on the pipes or the wires or the screens with a hammer and wrench and screwdriver—this was a dentist?—pronounce the problem fixed, and leave. If after three visits he still couldn't fix the problem, he said it was a mystery and nobody could.

Mornings when he couldn't make headway on his dissertation, Paul attempted some of the repairs himself, Maxine standing somewhere behind him, chewing on her nails and wincing. When he was at the point of cursing, she would say, "We can call Ed again. *I'll* call him if you like. Or we could call a real plumber. Pay for it ourselves. Paul? Paul?"

■ They tried everything to get their work done: switching offices; one going to the library half the day (usually Paul, who would come home in a panic, having accomplished nothing); wearing earplugs; disconnecting the phone; eating light, nutritious lunches and taking regular, well-planned breaks — methodical walks to the park nearby, or meditation sessions in the bedroom with the shades drawn (an instant failure due to the heat, Ann's bustling in with loads of laundry, and Josephine's bellowing at the window, "Is my mother there? MR. AND MRS. BABER!"). Often they would just give up and retreat to the bedroom anyway, making love and napping — between loads of laundry. "God damn her," Paul would say. "Is she stupid or what?"

"Stupid."

"We're newlyweds," he said. "What does she think we're doing in here?"

"Praying."

"Can't she hear us? Can't she figure it out?"

"No," Maxine said.

"For this we get to use a washer and dryer for free. I'd rather go to a laundromat."

"I'd rather wash it by hand," Maxine said.

They finally cornered Ann and spoke to her about arranging a laundry schedule, something reasonable they could all live with — on certain days at certain times. "Well," Ann said, "I guess I could ask my husband."

"Ask him what?" Maxine said once Ann had left, lugging the everpresent laundry basket on her hip.

"Oh," Paul waved his hand, "let her ask. I'm too hot to care anymore."

Both were perspiring from the dryer heaving out hot air all afternoon. And that squeaking! They'd tried WD-40, and a silicone spray recommended by the hardware store; they'd tried kicking the dryer, slapping it with their palms. They'd spoken to Ann, whose only idea on the subject was to speak to her husband about that too — maybe he could fix it. This husband the Babers hardly ever saw. He reportedly got up at 4:30 A.M., drove the hour and a half to Denver, worked at construction until God knows when, then stole back when everyone else was asleep. The only signs that he really existed were the knocking and grinding of the water pipes before dawn and the sight of him Sunday mornings hustling his family off to church.

They attended the Church of the Foursquare Gospel, on the other side of town. Maxine knew this from asking, casually of course. Ann confided that her husband, Drake, was studying to be a minister there.

"Drake?" Maxine said. "He's going to be a minister?"

"Once he gets his certificate," Ann continued, "he'll be a minister. Then we'll move. We'll build our own house. *He'll* build it."

Drake a minister. When Maxine told Paul, he couldn't believe it either. Though neither one had talked to him, they agreed that Drake was the most sullen and withdrawn man they'd ever seen. So flat and unyielding was the back of his square blond head, it was as if he'd been tied to a board as a youth. As far as they could see, Drake never played with Josephine, never held the baby, never talked to Ann or anyone else. Sunday afternoons he sat outside in a lawn chair, alone. Ann and the children were inside, watching TV, the sound of it coming up through the heating vents.

■ The Babers were now avoiding their own laundry. The closet in their bedroom, a long, deep, narrow, dark affair (the catacombs, they called it), was usually piled knee-deep in back with dirty clothes. They would undress and sling their shorts and T-shirts over the top of the bar from which hung shirts and dresses. Sometimes the clothes wouldn't make it and would hang there listlessly, like lost souls.

One afternoon, between Ann's loads of laundry, Maxine gathered up all the clothes in the back of the closet and stuffed them into a duffel bag. "I'm going to the laundromat," she told Paul. "Want to go?"

He was cleaning his computer screen with a cloth. "Sure," he said, "why not."

They drove to a laundromat they'd seen advertised in the paper — "totally air-conditioned," with wide-screen TVs, video games, and pinball machines amid the washers and dryers. While Maxine sorted clothes, Paul went across the street and bought a couple of beers.

"This is the place we should've rented," he said, once they were settled in front of the TV, cool for the first time all summer.

They took their time with the laundry, stayed for the news and a video game, and when later they pulled up in front of their house, Ann was sitting outside folding baby clothes. "So hot," she called out to them. "So awful hot." Fanning her thin, pink, freckled face. Oblivious to their duffel bag.

"Ann," Maxine said to her the next morning, unable to stand it anymore — the squeaking dryer, Josephine laughing demonically at her doll face-down in the pool — needing control over something! "Have you given any thought to a schedule? You know, for the laundry?"

"Oh." Ann brushed the hair from her eyes. Maxine saw a tiny bruise on the inside of her elbow. "I guess I forgot all about it, to tell you the truth. I'm just so tired with the baby and all. But we could do it anyhow you want. I don't want to bother you."

Now Maxine felt guilty. "Well, give it some thought. I don't know what your laundry needs are." Laundry needs?

"The other people who lived here," Ann said, "before you, were gone so much. It wasn't a problem then."

"It could be every other day. Or every day if you need to — just as long as we know when to expect you." Why had she said every day? That's what they were doing now. She'd only meant to sound flexible, reasonable.

Three days later, still no laundry schedule. Maxine asked Paul to please handle it. To go on like this — Ann skulking around with her laundry, knocking on their door to use her own washer and dryer, apologizing for bothering them but bothering them nonetheless — was unbearable.

"I don't think I got it across," she told Paul. "That *Ann* should come up with a schedule." Maxine didn't want to dictate to Ann when she could or could not do her laundry. "You talk to her."

"I will," he said. But he didn't. And Maxine didn't insist.

■ Late one afternoon when Paul was at the library, Maxine heard a knock on the front door. It was Ann. "I was wondering if it was okay with you if I used your phone," she said.

"Is yours broken?"

"Usually I just walk down to the store."

Maxine understood: they didn't have a phone. "Come in, come in," she said. "The phone's over there."

She went into her office and pretended to work at something, trying not to hear what was being said, but hearing anyway. Ann was talking to her minister. "He hasn't for a while now, no. But, Reverend . . . No." There was a pause. "No." Another. "No."

Maxine imagined the reverend, in a sports shirt, hefty and imperial, a glass of iced tea in his hand.

"I suppose so," Ann said. "Thank you, Reverend. Yes, I will."

Maxine heard her hang up the phone. Then there was silence, as if Ann were standing there utterly motionless. Maxine considered what she should do, if she should do anything. She poked her head out of her office. "Is everything okay?"

Ann was already scurrying toward the door.

"Would you like a Coke, or some tea?" Maxine said, immediately wondering why she'd asked. A perverse curiosity about Ann's life? Or pure loneliness? Most of her graduate school friends were away for the summer.

"Oh . . . I can't. The baby."

"Bring the baby here."

"Well." Ann looked anxiously at her. "All right. I guess that would be all right."

They sat at the kitchen table, Ann sipping tea with the baby on her lap, Maxine gamely attempting a few questions. How had she and Drake met? At church. How long till they'd married? A year. What was he like? Nice (nice?). Had they been members of the church long? Oh, years. Halting answers that revealed little beyond such details as what Drake preferred to eat for dinner, or that he snored, or that the rain last Sunday caused the roof at the church to leak.

Ann asked no questions. Not one. Apparently it made no difference to her that Maxine had a degree in sociology and that she would soon, if she could ever finish her thesis and defend it, obtain a master's in the same. Or that Paul and she had met at a consortium, fallen in love, and despite the shock of their colleagues, friends, and family— who never suspected them to be *that* type, so impulsive, Paul and Maxine? — married within a month.

And now Maxine feared that she was pregnant, yes, two months after the wedding. Her period was late. This she shared with Ann, briefly, matter-of-factly — maybe this was why she'd invited her for tea — while Ann breast-fed the baby and nodded as if this, pregnancy, she understood.

■ That night Maxine couldn't sleep, trying to guess whether or not she was pregnant. She counted on her fingers the days since her last period. Then she recounted based on the two times they'd made love without the diaphragm; she'd thought it had been safe then, but. But. She reviewed her symptoms — breast tenderness, leg pains, dizziness, ravenous hunger — and tried to recall everything she'd ever heard about the first month of pregnancy. Yes, she would think, I'm pregnant. Then she would think No, I'm not.

She wondered if she wanted to be pregnant. Yes, yes! Then fear, then shame — she should've been more careful. So early in their marriage: wouldn't this be a terrible mistake?

Maxine considered turning on the light to look at the calendar again; maybe she was wrong about being pregnant, or had counted wrong. Maybe she was a day off, and a day in this case could make a difference. No. She would wait until tomorrow. She must get some sleep now! Her thoughts shifted for some reason to Ann's minister, the reverend, wondering what they'd discussed on the phone. *He hasn't for a while now, no,* Ann had said. Hasn't what? Maxine tried to fill in the word. Hasn't touched me? Hasn't had a drink? Perhaps it had something to do with the ministry. Or maybe they weren't even discussing Ann's husband. Maybe it was a relative of hers, or the baby.

Maxine imagined the reverend on the phone, ordering people's lives according to God's plan. Shuffling them like a deck of cards. She pictured him in bed now, an inflated, hairy shape in white cotton pajamas, the reverend asleep on his back.

■ Josephine, though still obnoxious, was no longer totally impossible, the thrill of Mr. and Mrs. Baber having worn off. Now she would wait for them to finish their day's work, able to sense from any point in the yard, it seemed, the very moment of completion. At that instant she would knock on the door and ask to come in. To use the toilet. To look for her doll. To get away from her baby brother ("He's driving me crazy").

"Can I have a glass of water?" she asked one afternoon.

"What kind?" Paul said.

"What kind of *water?* There's only one kind."

"We have pink, green, blue ... "

"You do not."

He served her water tinted with food coloring. Josephine looked at the glass suspiciously while Paul drank his down — green water. "Ahh," he said. "Delicious. Care for some, my dear?" he asked Maxine.

"No, thank you."

"I'll be going then," he said, grabbing his wallet and car keys. Kissing Maxine on the lips. "Enjoy your water, Josephine."

"Where is he going?" she asked once he left. She no longer called them Mr. and Mrs. Baber, but *you, he, she, him, her.*

"Errands."

"Why aren't you going with him?"

"Because." The truth was she was waiting for the phone to ring, for the results of her pregnancy test.

Josephine stood up.

"Where are you going, Josephine?"

"Out," she said. Maxine followed her as far as the front window and saw her go to where Paul's car had been and look around, up and down the street.

The back door swung open: Ann dragging in the basket overflowing with sheets and towels. "This one's two loads, I think."

Still no laundry schedule. Ann had already been up here once today, and that load, her husband's shirts — a whole load of shirts! how did these people dirty so many clothes? — was squeaking rhythmically in the dryer.

Neither Paul nor Maxine had washed clothes in two weeks; yesterday they'd guiltily dropped off their laundry at a place that did it for you. Supposedly for busy people ... they'd tried to look busy and harassed as they handed over the duffel bag.

Ann propped her hands on her lower back. "Oh, I'm so tired. When is this going to end?"

Maxine wondered if she meant the laundry, the hot summer, or what — her marriage? servitude to life?

"Ann," she said. She was going to mention the laundry schedule again, then changed her mind. If she was pregnant they would move; or would they? Why did she assume they would move? "Ann."

Ann was sorting towels from sheets.

"Remember the laundry schedule? We still think it would be a good idea if ..."

Ann stood there hugging an armful of towels.

"Ann?" Maxine saw the tears running down her cheeks. At the same moment, the baby started screaming, as if he could sense from the basement his mother's grief. "Ann, are you all right?"

"It's nothing."

"Nothing? You're crying."

"Just some days I can't believe all this — " she dropped the towels in a heap. "All I'm doing is laundry and we don't have any money and I never see Drake anymore — "

The phone rang. Chances were it was the doctor's office with the test results. Maxine imagined running to the phone, the relief—or the sorrow?—of hearing that the test was negative.

"It's nothing really," Ann said, bending down to pick up the towels. "It's nothing. Aren't you going to answer your phone?" Irritation in her voice. "I have to get the baby anyhow," she said, her voice back to its normal monotone, the baby's screams rising as though he might tear himself apart.

■ Maxine was pregnant.

Maxine was not pregnant.

Incredibly, the doctor's office didn't know which at first. The test had been negative, but when her period still did not arrive and the symptoms continued, the test was repeated and this time was positive.

That made Maxine approximately two months pregnant. If she was pregnant. She still doubted it, no matter what the test said. She read an account in the paper of a woman who'd gone through an entire pregnancy, but when nine months were up, nothing happened. Ten months, still no baby, eleven months . . . The woman, it turned out, was not pregnant after all.

"But she was obese," Paul said, when she read him the article. "This can't happen to you."

It was difficult celebrating a pregnancy that was so elusive. First they'd gone out to dinner to celebrate that she wasn't pregnant. A few weeks later they were back at the same restaurant—not many fancy restaurants in a town this size—to celebrate the pregnancy.

Her friends, filtering back into town now for the fall term, were tentatively—everything about this was tentative—planning a baby shower for her, but Maxine couldn't even take pleasure in that. She secretly believed it was duty on their parts, not joy for her; they'd all thought her crazy for getting married so fast anyway, and now a baby . . .

If there was a baby. "Of course there is," Paul said. But even he seemed doubtful, despite the evidence: doctor appointments, her exhaustion and nausea. One night he actually suggested they use the diaphragm, just in case.

"Just in case!" she said, pushing him away. "If I wasn't pregnant, I certainly must be now." They'd been making love without birth control for weeks. "I know I'm pregnant, you know I'm pregnant, so let's get on with it."

"It was a joke," he said. "I was kidding."

"Were you."

"I'm glad you're pregnant."

She turned away from him, trying to shake off his hand, which remained resolutely on her shoulder, then her belly. She wished she could crawl inside of him: the baby in her, she in him, like nesting dolls. Who was he really? Her husband, but . . . now they were connected as never before, and for this frightening moment she didn't know who he was. Who she was with him.

The next morning she sat dully before her computer once again, her "Let's get on with it" of the night before mocking her as she stared at her incomplete thesis, her defense of it now seemingly delayed, everything now in suspended animation.

Only Ann seemed truly joyous and certain. "See?" she said after the second pregnancy test, showing Maxine the bright-blue baby blanket she'd been knitting all along. It was ugly, cheap-looking, but Maxine told her the blanket was beautiful.

"It's not done yet," Ann said, blushing, and hoisted the baby higher on her hip, his bald head after all these months still resembling a kind of skinned potato.

■ "Paul?"

He was getting ready for work.

"Remember you promised to speak to Ann about the laundry? You never did. I didn't call you on it because — well, I don't know why. But could you please talk to her? Especially if we're going to stay here." It was one of those days when she'd woken up certain she could go back to her old self: if she worked hard, she could finish her thesis within the month, possibly schedule her defense of it just before Christmas. "Paul, *do* you want to stay here?"

"Probably not." He was leafing through papers, stuffing some into his briefcase, his completing a draft of his dissertation and thus returning to work motivated in part by the second pregnancy test.

"We have the money now. Let's break our lease, let's move."

"Uh-huh."

"You're not listening." She felt herself about to burst into tears, but struggled against it—just her frustration, this not having anywhere to go in the mornings: like Ann now, except Maxine didn't bother with housework and certainly not laundry; instead, she sat around feeling sorry for herself. Or guilty about her thesis.

That night she tried again. "Since I am," she said, "pregnant, can't we please move? Get a place of our own? No neighbors?" She almost whispered as she said this, so aware was she of Ann and her family downstairs, the sounds and smells of dinner emanating from the heating vent. Josephine screaming. Baby screaming. Hamburger Helper, canned peas, rice. She felt a movement in her belly. The fetus squirming? Impossible. Too early yet. Her nerves, not the baby's. "Paul?"

By now it was fall, and the house was so drafty that they almost welcomed Ann's many loads of laundry; the dryer kept the apartment warmer, although it fogged the kitchen windows and cloaked the air so thickly with lint that Maxine believed she could taste it on the mornings she vomited.

They stayed. The house was cold, their heating bills high; they had to share a thermostat with the basement. Not to mention the bill, which Ann frowned over each time Maxine handed it to her. There were no storm windows, and after one early snowstorm, ice clung to the screens—making, Maxine told Paul, for a very depressing atmosphere, didn't he agree?

Oh yes.

But he wasn't ready to move yet.

"Why not?" Maxine asked. "You hate this place! You complain more than I do."

"I know." He drew her to him, another draft of his nearly completed dissertation on his lap between them; a long time since they'd held each other. "Why don't you look for a place?" he said. "Start looking?"

"Okay." But she didn't really, other than to drive around limply noting For Sale signs, the car like a boat, herself seasick. Never jotting down numbers, not calling, wishing only to sleep.

■ Ann and Drake had invited Paul and Maxine to dinner. Or rather, Ann had. Saturday evening at six, the Babers descended the front steps to the basement apartment, Maxine in a dress that barely fit across the belly, Paul wearing a tie, which he was already untying and stuffing into his pocket as they approached the door.

"I'm dreading this," he said under his breath. "Do we really have to do this?"

"Ditto," Maxine said. They leaned against each other and Paul knocked. Drake opened the door, nodding a greeting; he had on a frayed mustard-colored shirt Maxine recognized from yesterday's load of wash. With his knotted, stubby fingers, he handed them Cokes — she supposed they didn't drink — while Ann stood over a steaming, spitting frying pan and Josephine danced around the apartment twirling and showing off. Paul and Maxine glanced at each other: was it going to be like this?

"Where's the baby?" Maxine asked Ann.

"In there." She pointed, talking loudly over the pork chops. "Asleep. Finally." Rolling her eyes. "He's been up all day." These days she spoke to Maxine exclusively of topics related to babies: teething, how the first solid foods cause constipation, worries about ear infections — subjects Maxine didn't find particularly any more interesting than before she was pregnant. But what else did they have in common?

"Is he sleeping through the night yet?" she said, although she knew perfectly well he wasn't; the baby's cries woke them nearly every night.

Ann shook her head, and Maxine noticed she'd curled her bangs. Especially for tonight? To her knowledge, she and Paul were the couple's first dinner guests ever in this apartment — in honor of the coming baby, Ann had said. Maxine had never been inside before, only as far as the front door to hand Ann the gas bill. The apartment was very clean, very simple: a couch spread with a quilt backed against the wall, a coffee table, a card table set for four in the center of the room.

"Can I do anything to help?" she said.

Another shake of the bangs. They soon sat down to eat, whereupon Drake seized one of her hands, Ann the other.

"God," Drake said, "who gaveth his only son, Jesus of Nazareth, we thank thee for this food we are about to receive."

Ann raised her head. "Amen."

For an awful moment Maxine thought Drake and Ann were waiting for her and Paul to say "Amen" before lifting their forks. "This looks delicious," Maxine said, unfolding her napkin. "What kind of sauce is this?"

"Apple," Ann said. "I made it myself."

The sauce, as it turned out, was sickeningly sweet, and Maxine wondered how and if she could eat it. Josephine sat at the coffee table eating her own version of the meal: pork chop cut into pieces, applesauce; she was burying chunks of the meat in the sauce, then digging them out with her spoon. "Mommy." Her little wet lips were dribbling with milk and applesauce. "Mommy . . . "

Drake mumbled a question, and soon Paul was explaining what his job entailed.

"Mommy!" Josephine clambered to her feet and whispered in Ann's ear. She then ran toward the bathroom — or so Maxine assumed, since it was right under their bathroom. She was in there a long time.

Paul was still explaining, which for some reason annoyed Maxine. Perhaps it was jealousy, knowing that no one here would ask her anything except how she was feeling, less nauseous now, backache? Excited about the baby?

"When will you become a minister, Drake?" she asked. Paul shot her a look; they had agreed to avoid this subject, the whole subject of religion.

"In a year."

"What does it involve, becoming a minister?"

She scarcely listened to the answer, about the many hours of Bible study and being a deacon and so on, although she was gratified to hear something of what made this man proud. His whole face changed to a less sunken, more appealing, if not ethereal, expression.

Josephine, having returned from the bathroom, excavated some more pieces of pork chop from her applesauce with her spoon. She then picked up her plate and carried it off purposefully, as if to take it to the kitchen. Instead she turned into the baby's room. Maxine glanced at Ann to see if she noticed.

Paul was asking Drake about his faith, and it was Maxine's turn to shoot him a look. What exactly did Drake believe? What about his church, what were its tenets? Paul qualifying his questions with his own view, that organized religion was what people turned to when they couldn't accept that there were no absolutes, no answers. Drake blowing his nose violently in response, saying his was a church for people who had nothing else but their faith.

"Excuse me," Maxine said and got up to use the bathroom.

"I'll put on the coffee," Ann said. "Men," she said to Maxine as she followed her across the room, but her voice was tremulous, afraid.

In the bathroom Maxine noticed shampoo squirted all over the tub and toilet paper squished together in clumps like bouquets of flowers. Josephine. Maxine could hear Ann calling her now. "Josephine? What are you doing in there?"

Then quiet. No, a faint and desperate noise as if someone — Josephine? — were scratching at the wall between this room and the baby's. From the toilet she could see a word written almost microscopically on the edge of the molding: *Help*. Josephine was too young to write. Ann? A previous tenant?

Maxine leaned over her knees, feeling her belly, the source of all the chaos growing inside. "Baby baby baby." She'd say this to comfort herself sometimes, even before the pregnancy. She patted her stomach. "Baby baby."

She heard a scuffle on the other side of the wall, the baby's room. Drake's voice. "What are you doing!"

By the time Maxine got there, Drake was shaking the baby by the feet, upside down. Paul watched in horror. Ann was crying, Josephine whimpering, "He was hungry, he was hungry." Drake pressed his fingers below the baby's sternum and a piece of pork flew from the tiny mouth. Josephine wailed.

"You could've choked him!" Drake was shouting. "He was choking!"

Josephine hid behind her mother. "She was trying to help," Ann said.

"*You.* You stay out of this."

Paul motioned to Maxine for them to go. She looked at the baby, who blinked and sucked his fingers. She followed Paul out of the room.

"Wait," Ann said. At the door she handed them a package as Josephine clung to her legs. "You can probably guess what this is," she said. The poor thing was so nervous. Drake stood in the background holding the baby; he mumbled an apology and said goodnight.

It was the blanket. It was finished.

■ The following day, the Babers went to an open house in a condo development. "This is ridiculous," Maxine said, a color brochure in her hand. "We can't afford this."

"I know," Paul said, and moved off to speak with a real-estate agent. The place was crawling with them.

"May I answer any questions for you?" one said to Maxine. A woman.

"I'm pregnant," she said.

"So I see."

"I don't have any questions."

She read the brochure. Each condo had a view of the mountains, wall-to-wall carpeting, fireplace, dishwasher, trash compactor. Its own washer and dryer.

The development was called The Corners. Near a brand new shopping center and park, near schools and bicycle trails.

Maxine had dreams about it, back at their place, for the two more months they lived there — during which time they decided against a condo in favor of the small, white house with a yard — endless afternoon dreams while the baby cried in the basement, while Ann sorted laundry to be washed. While Paul completed his dissertation at last.

While her own thesis lay incomplete.

Like a long fever, these dreams: in one she and Paul were driving, the defroster going. Through fogged windows they saw chrome shopping carts and video stores, hungry children eating popcorn. Asphalt roofs and tiny vegetable gardens. Dreams of years and years of this, paying bills and minding children. Of everything breaking down, being fixed, then breaking down again ...

She woke up. Beside her on the bed Paul was reading a book on childbirth. He must've thought she was still asleep, so silently did he turn the pages, marking places with bits of colored paper. Maxine felt the baby kick and placed a hand on her belly, pretending for a moment it was someone else's hand. No. Impossible to feel this from the outside with her own fingertips when it was inside her, inside, the movement from within deep, quaking, satisfying. "Paul," she said, wanting to share it with him. "Paul." As though they'd been thrown to the earth and rooted there by grace of her womb, entangled with the other plants and creatures.

THE GRAND TOUR

My mother would make me go there, to see Jennifer Wakely and her sister, Alice. They lived in a mansion over by the Arroyo Seco and had only heard of San Marino, the town nearby where I lived; they'd never actually been there.

The Arroyo Seco was in South Pasadena, the wealthiest part, wealthier even than San Marino — steep hills and winding roads paved so smooth and black I was afraid my mother's Mercedes-Benz would glide right over the edge. Her driving was awful. Fortunately she managed to stay on the road, past iron-gated entrances with carved stone lions and tall, pointing cypresses. "This, Cynthia," my mother would say, "reminds me of Italy. What do you think?"

"I've never been there, Mother." She'd never been there either.

"But you've seen pictures?"

"Yes." I said, glum as possible, hoping she'd change her mind about taking me there — to Jennifer and Alice's.

Jennifer was my age exactly, ten years old, and the one my mother had earmarked to be my friend. She and her sister looked alike, only Alice was two years older and starting to develop. Both had sickly blond hair, so limp you could see the places where the maid had stuck in the bobby pins. And both had a profusion of blond fuzz on their skinny arms and legs, like rare blond monkeys in smocked dresses.

They never wore pants or shorts, only those dresses with puffed sleeves and sashes that tied in back. And stiff white oxfords. Not even saddle shoes, like I wore. The first day I met them I lifted my skirt to prove I had on shorts under my dress. Jennifer and Alice looked shocked.

"It's so I can play kickball at school," I explained. "All the girls do it. So the boys can't see your underwear."

"Hedwig would never let us do that," Jennifer said.

Hedwig was the maid.

They didn't say much about their parents.

■ Playing with Jennifer, my mother called these visits. Each Thursday after school she'd meet me in the parking lot, her sunglasses on, the Mercedes humming. "Hurry up, Cynthia," she'd say, opening the door and shooing me inside. "You don't want to keep Jennifer waiting, do you?"

"I don't want to go there, Mother. Why do I have to go there? I have friends." And they were a lot more fun than Jennifer, I wanted to say.

"And it's always nice to make new friends," my mother said, "I think so."

She always talked like that on Thursdays, en route to Jennifer and Alice's: her honey voice, which meant I'd better not cross her. Which meant I'd better go without complaint.

Sometimes I said, "Can't we go feed the ducks instead?"

"With Jennifer?"

"No, not with Jennifer. Just us." Back in the good old days, before I turned ten and before my mother started her campaign to introduce me to the right people, the only times we went to the Arroyo Seco were to feed the ducks at a pond my mother knew about, somebody's private pond.

"You're a little old for that now," my mother said.

■ Playing with Jennifer meant playing with Alice, too. Alice didn't have any friends of her own.

Here's how it went: my mother would pull into their driveway, the half-moon kind with a portico attached to the house — a pink brick mansion that always reminded me of chopped salmon. Sometimes a man with oiled hair would appear from behind the front door to help me out of the car; sometimes he just watched us slyly from a window, as if not in the mood.

At other times, Jennifer and Alice's mother would rush out to meet us, on her way to somewhere else — a car would pull up, the man driving it would hop out and she in. "Monica!" she'd say to my mother. Mrs. Wakely, as I was taught to greet her ("Hello, Mrs. Wakely, how are you today?"), didn't seem to know my name. "Oh, hello, dear," she'd say over the top of my head without actually looking at me.

Sometimes there was no one to watch me or meet me. My mother would simply drop me off. "You're going to have lots and lots of fun," she'd say. "I promise! I'll be back in two hours." And away she drove, leaving me on the Wakelys' doorstep all alone.

If the man wasn't around, nor Mrs. Wakely, I'd ring the bell and wait. At last Jennifer would open the door. "It's Cynthia," she'd say to Alice. "Well, come in."

One reason I hated going to the Wakelys' is that we did the same thing every time for the entire five or six months I had to go there. We went on a tour of the house. Jennifer would take my hand, Alice would clasp *her* hand, and we'd go room by room.

"This is the kitchen," Jennifer would say. "My mother doesn't cook here because we have a cook."

Their stove was enormous, the kind you'd see in a restaurant, with twelve burners. There were about a hundred pots and pans hanging from hooks all over the kitchen.

"They're burned," I said the first time. "Doesn't your cook know how to clean anything? They're black!"

"That's the way they're supposed to be," Jennifer said. "They're cast iron. And the cook doesn't wash dishes. We have a maid to do that."

"Hedwig?"

"No, she's *our* maid."

She showed me the pantries and the dumbwaiter and the dishwasher and the inside of the refrigerator — which opened up like a birthday card with three panels — and we peered into the deep freeze at the meats wrapped in white paper and marked with red pen. I wanted something to eat, a cookie, but was too nervous to ask.

"What's in that room?" I said. There was a high counter with little swinging doors that led out to somewhere.

"Just a minute," Jennifer said. "We have to go down to the laundry first."

"No!" Alice said.

"It's all right, Alice. There's nobody down there."

There was nobody around anywhere, that day and nearly all the other times I went there. Except for that man who hung around the front door. The others, the maids, the cook, the gardener, and the rest of them, must've started their day early and been taking a break, or else they were hiding, secretly watching our tour. Or maybe the house ran itself. It was very mysterious, and I could understand why Alice was afraid: the Wakelys' house was scary.

Their laundry was in the basement, not just a washer and dryer, but two of each, and a total of three rooms all connected by passageways. There were chutes where the laundry came down (from the fourth floor even, Jennifer said). And some ironing boards that pulled out from the wall (Jennifer demonstrated) and wonderful-smelling wicker baskets and a few canvas carts with black rubber wheels. I was hoping to roll them around and have races, but Jennifer said it was time to go.

We went upstairs a different way, opening a door and climbing a wooden spiral staircase. "This is the way the maids go," Jennifer said.

It was pitch black and poor Alice was sniffling and clearing her throat—to make it not seem so lonely, I guess. I patted her shoulder and sang a song I'd learned at school. "My hat it has three corners, three corners has my hat . . ."

"Shh," Jennifer said. "You're not supposed to talk on this stairwell."

She pushed open a door and now we stood in a hallway with a thick Persian rug. I followed her and Alice into another room and recognized the little swinging doors I'd asked about earlier. "This is the dining room," Jennifer said. "We eat here every night, at seven-thirty. The cook pushes the food through those doors and Jackie serves it to us."

Jackie, I was to learn, was the man who sometimes helped me out of my mother's car and sometimes hid behind the window to spy on me.

"This table," Jennifer said, "has a leaf in it. Do you know what that is?"

"Yes."

"It makes the table larger. In case we have guests. Sometimes there are thirty people. When that happens, my mother uses the silver." She pointed to a silver tea service that gleamed like a deformed sort of mirror. "There's more inside this buffet," Jennifer said, showing me, "and more in the pantry where we keep such things, the Imari china and so on."

I was getting bored. But this was only the beginning, I found out.

■ I only met Hedwig once, although sometimes when our tour passed her room, I could hear her chair squeaking in front of a TV set.

She was German and had blotches on her face and didn't like me — or Jennifer and Alice, it seemed.

"Out! Out!" was what she said the time I met her, when the tour stopped at her door and knocked.

"Hedwig," Jennifer said, "I'd like you to meet my friend Cynthia Norris."

"Hello," Hedwig said. "Now go play."

Jackie was a different story. I could feel his presence always, could feel him watching us, even when Jennifer claimed he was out on an errand.

"Is he German?" I asked her once.

"We don't know what he is," she said.

Their father, Mr. Wakely, I never met.

"He's at work," Jennifer always said.

"What's he do?"

"Business."

But she offered to show me his portrait. In fact, this was a regular stop on the tour, a sitting room with paintings and photographs of the family.

"This was my grandmother," Jennifer would say as we stood beneath an oil painting of a woman and a dog. And so on — portraits of her other grandparents and her aunts and uncles; there was even one of Jennifer and Alice as very small children under a tree, much prettier than they were in real life.

Alice enjoyed that one especially. While Jennifer led me around the room, Alice would stand gazing at their portrait, smiling curiously and holding her hands up like paws, one higher than the other, as though she might wave at the two little girls. "I remember that day," she'd say to Jennifer, or to herself. "Do you?"

"These are pictures of our father," Jennifer would say when the sitting room portion of the tour was nearly over. "Don't touch the frames. They'll tarnish."

One photo showed him standing outside the church on his wedding day, looking at his watch, a smile playing on his lips.

"He's handsome," I said the first time I saw it.

"Yes," Jennifer said, while Alice stooped slightly behind her, rubbing her nose with the sash of her dress.

The rest of the tour included guest bedrooms and bathrooms, hallways, a real library with books, and a formal living room with striped silk couches that reminded me of Christmas candy. "In summer," Jennifer would say, "we change the slipcovers to something lighter, more pearl-colored."

From there we'd go upstairs to view the family bedrooms. We'd start with Jennifer's, then on to Alice's, the two rooms connected by French doors hung with lace and dotted swiss.

"These doors open all the way," Jennifer said, "so that our rooms become a playroom."

But she never opened the doors. We hardly spent any time in their rooms at all, despite the dolls and stuffed animals and games to play. The most Jennifer would allow was a peek inside her closet.

"This is where I keep my dresses," she'd say. "See? To get to my shoes, Hedwig has to climb a stepladder."

Alice would be silent during all this, sometimes looking about as though not quite sure where she was, and I felt sorry for her — the way her mouth gaped open and her nose was always pink around the edges. She had a rash on her legs, too, behind her knees, that Jennifer was forever telling her not to scratch. Jennifer told Alice how to do everything, even though she was younger. "Alice didn't know how to ride a bike," she told me once. "I taught her."

But we never rode bikes when I was there.

We did often linger by the doors of their parents' bedroom suite, decorated in the palest peach I'd ever seen. The bedside lamps, made of brass, were always on. "We're not allowed to go in there," Jennifer would say.

The best part of the tour was the attic on the fourth floor. There was a stage up there, built of pine and stained dark, the knots like black smudged eyes. There was even a red velvet curtain, and costumes, which on rare occasions Jennifer would let us try on.

"We could have a play," I said once or twice, hopefully.

"Yes!" Alice said.

But Jennifer said that wouldn't be a good idea.

■ There were arguments at night, the hallway door between my room and my parents' room firmly closed so it could be said I had never heard them fight. About the Arroyo Seco, about living there. It wasn't the money, my father would say. It was the waste, the frivolity. The emptiness of it all. *Emptiness?* said my mother, bursting into eerie laughter, and I would picture her, laughing to the point of spitting, coughing.

Yet the next morning she would smile at me triumphantly, as if she and I had won a great battle. "Someday, Cynthia," she would begin grandly, ignoring my father, who was also ignoring her, "when you and Jennifer are debs at Las Madrinas ..."

I wasn't going to be a debutante. I thought it was silly and, more important, so did my father, who thought it outrageous, spending that kind of money for a week of your life, when you could buy a car or so many shares of General Electric, or travel to Europe, even.

It was the same thing, Daddy said, as weddings. Lavish weddings with three hundred, four hundred guests, receptions at the California Club downtown.

He and my mother had eloped — for which she never forgave him.

She'd expected something else, she told me. A different sort of life, a different life — for *me*, she always stressed.

My mother had a copy of the Blue Book, though my father didn't know. The *Social Registry of Southern California*. He would've laughed. The Blue Book on her lap, my mother would ask for the spellings of my classmates' names, my friends' names.

"Mother, their names aren't in the Blue Book."

On would go her reading glasses; she paid me no heed.

"They're not in the Blue Book!"

"How do you spell Martin? With an 'i' or an 'e'?"

I'd clap my hands over my ears. "I don't care! Leave me alone!"

"Honey." She'd set the book aside. "Come here." She held me close. "I was only curious. Is it a sin to be curious?"

At other times my mother would lose interest in me altogether. Lose interest in everything. She'd sleep late, let the house go, spend long hours cutting her hair a new way, then have to go to the beauty shop to have it redone. I wasn't supposed to tell my father.

But he wasn't fooled, about this or anything else. Once when my mother was having one of her crying jags, my father took me out to the yard. "You have to be patient with your mother," he said. "She didn't have it easy as a child, you know." I knew. Her mother had died when she was a girl. It had been explained to me countless times.

Just as on countless Saturday mornings my father would complain, "This house is too empty. Cynthia, make more noise!"

To which my mother would coldly glance at him over the newspaper.

Those were our Saturday mornings: Daddy wishing to be entertained by family life, my mother distant, bored, irritated. As though my father were a hopelessly stupid stranger she'd encountered and now was stuck with.

She treated me that way too, at times. "Hurry up, Cynthia, come on" — dragging on a cigarette, waiting for me by the Mercedes. A trip to the store for white candles. She must, she would decide on a moment's notice, *must* have white candles. And I must accompany her. Now. Drop everything. "Could we show some enthusiasm, please?" she would say. As if by not snapping to it and running out to the car, I was somehow holding her back in life.

■ Sometimes when I visited the Wakelys', Alice and I would be left standing alone together while Jennifer was using the toilet, or when she answered the phone: "The Wakely residence. No, I'm sorry, ma'am, Mrs. Wakely isn't home. This is her daughter Jennifer. Would you care to leave a message?" Or we'd be left alone when Jennifer would suddenly announce, "I'll be back in a minute. Wait here." And off she went — I never knew where — as if it were very important.

I never knew what to say to Alice. "Do you like living here?" I asked her once.

"Yes," she said. "Don't you wish *you* lived here?"

It wasn't what I'd expected her to say. "But you don't seem to like it here," I said.

"That's not true," she answered.

Alice, I learned, could be extremely haughty. And bossy. But only when Jennifer wasn't around.

"You never say anything when she's around," I said. "How come?"

"I don't have to talk if I don't want to."

"Don't you like Jennifer?"

"Of course I do," she said. "Don't you?"

I became slightly afraid of her. I didn't understand how one moment she could be clinging to Jennifer and the next, digging her nails into my arm. "You little prick," she said to me once, at the exit of the staircase the maids used; Jennifer had left us there to close up the laundry room properly, she said.

I knew what the word *prick* meant.

"Why do you want to scare me?" I asked her.

"I don't know." Her eyes fluttered around so gracefully I thought maybe I'd imagined it, this way she had of acting sometimes. "I didn't mean to," she said. "Am I scaring you?"

"No." I watched her gazing at the other staircase, the main one with the curlicue banisters that went sweeping up the center of the house. "Let's hide from Jennifer," I said, grabbing her arm and pulling her upstairs. "Hide and seek!" I called out to Jennifer, from a closet on the second floor. "Come find us!"

She found us in an instant. "You don't belong in here," she said. "This is where the extra linens are kept."

Alice was sniffling and clearing her throat, the way she always did in dark places.

Hide and seek, as it turned out, was the only game Jennifer could be induced to play, although she did so reluctantly. "All right," she'd say. "But don't make a mess."

My favorite place to hide was the kitchen. There were all kinds of cabinets and large drawers and other small spaces to scrunch up into. Even though I hid there regularly, neither Jennifer nor Alice would think to look there first. I could hear one or the other of them in the living room or out in the sitting room with the portraits — no place to hide there, so I wondered why they bothered. "Cynthia? Oh Cynthia! Where are you?" At times I couldn't hear them at all (often it was only me hiding because Alice was afraid of being alone) and would realize they'd gone upstairs to search for me, and it could be hours before they'd find me. And so I would listen to the dripping faucet, the one Jennifer said the handyman had fixed a thousand times.

Jennifer always hid in the same place: behind one of the striped couches in the living room. We'd find her on her stomach, face-down.

"Why don't you try and make a break for it?" I'd say. As long as you weren't tagged, you weren't caught. You could run off and hide somewhere else.

"Oh," she'd say. "I forgot. I don't like this game anyway."

It was Alice, though, when she wasn't feeling afraid, who hid in the best places. She curled up inside the dryer; she squeezed herself into the buffet that held the silver; she stood on the windowsill in her parents' suite, behind the drapes ("You know you're not supposed to be in here," Jennifer said).

One time she hid in the first-floor laundry chute, holding on by her fingertips and, when she heard us coming, sliding down to the basement. Jennifer was furious, practically in tears. "You could've hurt yourself," she said. "And then what? Oh, let's not play this ever again!"

But we did.

One Thursday when my mother dropped me off, the man Jackie let me in the door. "Where are Jennifer and Alice?" I said.

"They're hiding, miss."

He was edging toward a door, the door to the tiny room he hid in, peeking out the window, when he didn't feel like helping me out of the car.

"Hiding, miss. They said to tell you. Hide and seek."

I'd never seen him up close before. He was small and hunched and his face appeared carved. The only thing smooth about him was his oiled hair, and I wondered what would happen if you dabbed it with a napkin.

He smiled. "Would you like some jellybeans?"

"I don't know."

"Sure you do, miss. Come in here."

I peeked inside his room; it was pale green with a table and chair and a small TV set.

"Come inside," he said. "It's all right."

But I wouldn't.

"Are you nice to them?" I said, meaning Jennifer and Alice.

"They're good girls," he said. "But everybody else here, you know. Okay. Not so nice."

"Are you German?" I thought all Germans were evil.

"No, miss. Now put out your hand for jellybeans." I did and he filled it to the brim. "They're hiding, miss. They're waiting. You go find them."

■ I searched the house, eerily quiet except for the high-pitched whine of Hedwig's TV set. "Jennifer! Alice! Jennifer! Alice!" I checked the laundry, the kitchen, the living room and sitting room, as well as all of Alice's favorite hiding places and even some she hadn't thought of yet.

I went into their parents' bedroom suite, not because I expected to find them — Jennifer would never allow it — but just because. I sat on the bed, opened some drawers, inspected their private bathrooms: who were they, Mr. and Mrs. Wakely? I peered into their toilets and wastepaper baskets. Not a trace, not a thread or a particle of dust.

Then I heard laughter from somewhere. Or maybe I imagined it. I ran through the house following the sound, afraid. By the time I got to the third floor I could hear them giggling on the fourth. "I hear you!" I yelled. "I'm coming!"

Then it was silent. Just as I reached the attic, there was a crash.

"Damn you, Alice!"

"Where are you?" I called out.

"Shut up. Here she comes."

Silence again. I climbed the rest of the stairs and this is what I saw: Jennifer and Alice on stage, in heavy makeup and long skirts and turbans, holding out empty plates. On the floor was a ladder, tipped over, and a bunch of fruit spilled everywhere, and an empty basket.

"Oh," I said.

"Can we stop this now?" Jennifer said. She took Alice's plate, stacked it on top of her own, and set the plates on the floor as if they belonged there.

"What are you doing?" I asked.

"It's done now," Jennifer said. "It's a tableau, or it was until Alice knocked over the ladder. I don't care. It was her idea anyway."

"I was just rearranging the fruit," Alice said.

"A tableau of what?" I said.

"Just a tableau," Alice said. "You know, where you don't move. It was supposed to be a surprise." She was sniffling, her usual sounds, I thought, but then I realized she was weeping. "You found us," she said. "I never thought you would."

I couldn't tell if she was glad or not.

"Oh, Alice," Jennifer said, "quit crying. It's messy enough as it is up here."

"Please don't be mad," Alice said. "Jennifer?"

"Don't Jennifer me." It was such a grown-up thing to say, something old people said to each other. And she did look old in that long skirt and turban. "I should have never let you talk me into this," she said. "Look at this mess! Look at it!" Now *she* was almost in tears.

"It's all right," I said. "Everything's all right. It's just some fruit on the floor. We can clean it up."

"It's not all right," Jennifer said. "You don't know what you're talking about, you don't understand."

I tried to touch her shoulder. I'd never seen her so upset.

"Leave me alone. I'm going downstairs. You made this mess, Alice. You clean it up!"

I helped Alice collect all the fruit, which had rolled off in different directions. Some of the grapes were squashed; I wiped them off the floor with the hem of my skirt. Then we put the plates back where they belonged, and the ladder, and the attic looked as empty as always.

"There," I said, but Alice said nothing.

I watched her take off the dress-up clothes and put on her smocked dress; her underwear was white cotton, just like mine, except she had hers pulled way up over her belly button.

"Don't look at me," she said.

"Sorry," I said. She was back to being haughty again.

"Now you can look."

She was holding up her skirt. Underneath she had on a pair of dark blue bloomers.

"Where did you find those?" I asked.

"Up here. This afternoon. I'm going to keep them and not take them off."

"Why?" I couldn't imagine Alice playing kickball.

"This way," she said, "nobody can see you." She twirled around in a circle. "When you grow up, you get hair down there. Did you know that?"

"Yes." I knew my mother had hair.

"And you bleed."

"I know." But I didn't understand why, not really.

"There's something else," she said.

She sat down beside me cross-legged, her eyebrows dark and smeared with pencil, her eyelids blue. "Sometimes Daddy goes to Jennifer's room. It's always at night. I can hear it — "

"Hear what?" I said. I didn't sound like myself; I sounded like my mother, like Jennifer. I thought of a girl I went to school with whose name I didn't know, a slow girl with huge knuckles and a bulging forehead. "Hear what?"

Alice brought my wrist to her mouth. "Don't be stupid," she said.

Very slowly she opened her mouth. I waited for her to say something.

"What?" I said.

I felt her lips, which were wet, moving against my wrist, then her tongue, then her teeth.

"Stop it!" I jumped away from her and stood up.

Her hands were over her ears now, her eyes shut tight. "I said I can hear it!" Her voice made me think of something ragged. "You know what I mean," she said.

I didn't know.

Downstairs I said goodbye to Jennifer, now dressed in her regular clothes, her face raw from rubbing off the makeup.

"Thank you for having me," I said at the door. "I'm sorry about the tableau."

"It's quite all right," Jennifer said in her most adult manner. "These things happen."

"Jennifer?" I held out my hand; it looked like wood.

"You're late, you know," she said. "Your mother's been waiting."

Jackie helped me into the Mercedes this time.

"Alice is crying," I told him. "In the attic."

He opened the door with a mock bow. "Goodbye young lady goodbye Cynthia," he said without pause between the words, as though announcing a song, and I knew then I would never go back.

■ At home that night I wouldn't eat dinner or talk to either of my parents. "What's wrong?" my mother asked. "Did you and Jennifer have a fight? Tell me."

I couldn't answer. Finally she put me to bed. "Don't touch me," I said when she leaned over to kiss me.

She drew away. "If you wish."

Soon I heard them arguing again, my father's voice tired and hopeless, my mother's mocking, persistent. Then angry, full of tears. It wasn't about the Arroyo Seco anymore. I didn't know what it was about, but each night it resumed, their voices sticking together and pulling apart like glue. White glue is how I pictured it that night, spinning me in a cocoon until I could sleep.

I woke up screaming — hair — blood — Jennifer's father did something at night —

"A bad dream." My mother was sitting at the end of the bed, her forehead in her hands.

"It's not a dream, Alice said — "

"Children." She was crying.

I thought about her mother dying, about Jennifer and Alice. I was afraid to speak.

"Children," she said. "Their little scrapes and bruises. I wish I had it back. It's nothing compared to this."

Later that year my father divorced her. She resisted, she clung to him, and at last she gave up. I felt I was to blame. My mother seemed to blame me also, subtly at first, with a look, a glance — for what I do not know. She asked that I not live with her; I would be much happier with my father, she told me. He and his new wife — he was remarried within the year — decided after a short time that I would be happier in boarding school. I thought this situation would change when my mother remarried, but it didn't, and in the long run I was relieved and thankful to be away at school.

■ I was pregnant with my first child when I saw Alice again, on a street in Pasadena.

Her hair was as blond as ever, its limpness disguised by the chignon she wore. Red woolen dress, black patent-leather belt, hard glittery diamonds on her fingers, lacquered nails.

"Alice?" For a minute I thought it must be Jennifer, from the way she turned — as though we were about to be formally introduced at a dinner party. "It *is* Alice," I said, "Alice Wakely? It's Cynthia Norris. Remember me?"

"I believe so." Her eyes strayed to the window display behind us, a camera store. "Yes, I remember you now."

I gathered she wasn't bowled over to see me, or even curious enough to ask questions — do you live around here? it's been years! a baby! your first? — but I said anyway, "How are you? How's Jennifer?"

"Oh," she said, "Jennifer is fine."

From the way her eyes returned to the camera store, I doubted it.

"Is she?" I said.

"Why, yes."

"What about you?"

"Fine."

We stood there awkwardly. "It seems funny," I said, "that I haven't run into you before. Or Jennifer." It wasn't at all strange; during college and for a time afterward I'd lived out of state.

"Oh, we're around," Alice said. Then she laughed. A wealthy woman's laugh, throaty and unsettling.

I persisted. "What is Jennifer up to these days?"

"Oh," she said once again — as if she wanted to think about it some. "She's married. Aren't we all."

"Any children? Either of you?"

"Yes. Both of us . . ." Her voice trailed off.

I learned a little more, through grilling her: that both she and Jennifer had a child each, girls; that neither had graduated from college; that both had married well — one husband a lawyer, the other a stock analyst.

"Remember how we used to go on tours around your house?" I said, watching her face. "Hide and seek? The tableau?"

A blank. She was about to say no, I think, when Jennifer herself walked out of the camera store. She was blond and elegant, dressed in black, followed by a small, dark-haired child about three or four years old.

"Alice!" I said. "Why didn't you tell me Jennifer was here?"

Alice snapped open her purse and took out a cigarette, which she didn't light.

Noticing me, Jennifer halted, waiting, apparently, for me to go up to her. "Cynthia," she said, without smiling. "This is my daughter, Marcy. Marcy, I'd like you to meet an old friend of mine, Cynthia Norris."

The little girl held out a tiny gloved hand. I thought it was gloved, at first. Then I saw it was unusually white and creamy, and somewhat bluish, as though underwater. She was beautiful. Everything around me seemed to shift, to undulate. I felt faint, from not having had lunch yet, from being pregnant; the girl spoke to me, and for a moment she and I were swimming toward each other in secret, our hands gliding, about to touch. "Hello," she said.

WESTERN LITERATURE SERIES

Western Trails: A Collection of Short Stories by Mary Austin
selected and edited by Melody Graulich

Cactus Thorn
Mary Austin

Dan De Quille, the Washoe Giant: A Biography and Anthology
prepared by Richard A. Dwyer and Richard E. Lingenfelter

Desert Wood: An Anthology of Nevada Poets
edited by Shaun T. Griffin

The City of Trembling Leaves
Walter Van Tilburg Clark

Many Californias: Literature from the Golden State
edited by Gerald W. Haslam

The Authentic Death of Hendry Jones
Charles Neider

First Horses: Stories of the New West
Robert Franklin Gish

Torn by Light: Selected Poems
Joanne de Longchamps

Swimming Man Burning
Terrence Kilpatrick

The Temptations of St. Ed and Brother S
Frank Bergon

The Other California: The Great Central Valley in Life and Letters
Gerald W. Haslam

The Track of the Cat
Walter Van Tilburg Clark

Shoshone Mike
Frank Bergon

Condor Dreams and Other Fictions
Gerald W. Haslam

A Lean Year and Other Stories
Robert Laxalt

Cruising State: Growing Up in Southern California
Christopher Buckley

The Big Silence
Bernard Schopen

Kinsella's Man
Richard Stookey

The Desert Look
Bernard Schopen

Winterchill
Ernest J. Finney

Wild Game
Frank Bergon

Lucky 13: Short Plays about Arizona, Nevada, and Utah
edited by Red Shuttleworth

The Measurable World
Katharine Coles

Keno Runner
David Kranes

TumbleWords: Writers Reading the West
edited by William L. Fox

From the Still Empty Grave: Collected Poems
A. Wilber Stevens

Strange Attraction: The Best of Ten Years of ZYZZYVA
edited by Howard Junker

Wild Indians & Other Creatures
Adrian C. Louis

Bad Boys and Black Sheep: Fateful Tales from the West
Robert Franklin Gish

Stegner: Conversations on History and Literature
Wallace Stegner and Richard W. Etulain

Warlock
Oakley Hall

The Iris Deception
Bernard Schopen

Low Tide in the Desert: Nevada Stories
David Kranes

Flying Over Sonny Liston: Poems
Gary Short

Just Past Labor Day: Selected and New Poems, 1969–1995
Kirk Robertson

A History of the Garden: Poems
Katharine Coles

Breathe Something Nice: Stories
Emily Hammond